# TO TAKE ARMS

# TO
# TAKE ARMS

## My Year with the
## IRA
## Provisionals

## Maria McGuire

THE VIKING PRESS
New York

# Contents

Prologue   *3*
1 † A Tradition of Discontent   *5*
2 † Commitment to a Cause   *12*
3 † Provisional Politics   *26*
4 † Gun-Running on the Continent   *36*
5 † Another Glorious Failure   *53*
6 † An Offensive Campaign   *72*
7 † The New Year Border War   *80*
8 † Bloody Sunday   *92*
9 † Loyalist Backlash   *100*
10 † Counterproductive Casualties   *109*
11 † New Republican Myths   *119*
12 † Truce   *132*
13 † A Position of Strength   *147*
14 † Conflict as Usual   *153*
15 † Disenchantment and Escape   *165*
Epilogue   *176*
Chronology   *179*

# ILLUSTRATIONS

Sean Mac Stiofain  *23*

Ruairi O Bradaigh  *23*

David O'Connell  *38*

Maria McGuire  *38*

Bloody Sunday in Derry  *96*

The British Embassy in Dublin
after Fire-bombing  *97*

Bloody Friday in Belfast  *157*

# TO TAKE ARMS

# Prologue

*. . . for me the ultimate betrayal
would be to remain silent.*

I am, I suppose, a defector. I have left my family, my friends and
the movement I believed in—the Provisional IRA. But defectors
in the cold war between East and West always find another
country to welcome them. There is no such sanctuary for me.
The Provisional IRA believes that I have betrayed the movement in its fight against British economic and military control
of Ireland. But in leaving the Provisionals I have not gone over
to the British. I am still as opposed to their methods and policies in Ireland as ever. I am now effectively a stateless person.

I spent a year working with the Provisional IRA. I believed
in its aim of a new Ireland, free and, we hoped, united. I also
agreed with the Provisionals' methods. I supported the shooting of British soldiers and believed that the more who were
killed the better. I remember occasions when we heard late at
night that a British soldier had been shot and seriously wounded
in Belfast or Derry—and we would hope that by the morning he would be dead. I accepted too the bombing of Belfast,
and, when civilians were accidentally blown to pieces, dismissed this as one of the unfortunate hazards of urban guerrilla
war. In 1971 I went to Amsterdam with David O'Connell, then
a member of the Provisionals' ruling Army Council, to try to

buy arms and ammunition for the movement to continue its campaign.

My attitude towards the aims of the Provisional IRA has not changed. But I no longer consider that its methods are justified. My first doubts came in the spring of 1972, when Provisionals began shooting at unarmed Protestants in the streets of Belfast, actions that could only hasten the slide to sectarian civil war in the Six Counties. I put these doubts to one side in June, when the Provisionals negotiated a truce with the British and achieved the strongest position the IRA has held in fifty years. But in July the truce collapsed; and then came Bloody Friday, when eleven civilians were killed and more than one hundred injured by twenty Provisional bombs that exploded in an hour. This was the end for me. There was no way such horror could bring the British back to the negotiating table. Yet the Provisionals could devise no alternative to this mindless, senseless killing. I knew too that no change in Provisional policy could come about while it was in the hands of Sean Mac Stiofain, the Army Council Chief of Staff. Mac Stiofain had eliminated all those Army Council members who opposed his policies and was now conducting a sterile and murderous campaign with equal ruthlessness.

For these reasons, I decided to come to Britain to tell what I knew about the way the Provisionals have been conducting their campaign. I know that many members of the Provisional movement consider me a traitor. But for me the ultimate betrayal would be to remain silent.

# 1

# A Tradition
# of Discontent

*All Ireland had
were symbols of freedom.*  . . .

There was no Irish Republican tradition in my family. My father was a civil servant and rose steadily through the Irish
Ministry of Agriculture over a period of twenty years. We
talked about politics together, but nearly always on a theoretical basis, and usually about other countries, especially America
and France. We lived in a comfortable modern semi-detached
house in the Dublin suburb of Churchtown, to the south of the
city. I had two brothers and one sister, all younger than I.

My mother had been raised as a good Catholic, and I was
naturally brought up as a Catholic too. My mother wanted me
to succeed at all aspects of school life, and I was always preco-
cious there, going into the class above my own age group, coming high up in most subjects, and being good at games too. At
ten I entered Saint Anne's Secondary School in Milltown,
where all the teachers were nuns. At the age of twelve I decided I could no longer accept the doctrines of the Catholic
Church. There were questions in my mind which I was ready to
have answered. But the Catholic priests who came to talk to us

were halting and ineffectual and could never answer even the most straightforward question about the dilemmas of their religion. They always resorted to talking of the "mysteries" of the Catholic Church and how it was necessary to "have faith." My renunciation horrified the school, which assumed that I was either mad or a Communist. I stopped going to Mass, which upset my parents, but as liberals they accepted my decision.

But I still worked very hard at Saint Anne's and enjoyed most classes, especially English, Latin, history, and French. Latin had a logical beauty about it, and the language came easily to me—my father had liked it too, which was perhaps an additional impetus. I often got up at five in the morning to study, and arrived at school at seven-thirty, let myself in, and sat in the empty classroom to read. By going to school so early, too, I could avoid travelling on the crowded rush-hour buses, which I hated.

I liked games and was captain of the lower-school teams at netball and hockey. But I didn't socialize much and at home hardly ever went out until I was fourteen or fifteen. I didn't like parties, and I didn't enjoy meeting people. I often stayed up to read until midnight or later, and my parents would have to beg me to go to bed. For a long time I wanted to act. I enjoyed displaying emotion on the stage—something I found strangely difficult in real life. I remember my mother telling me that to show emotion was a sign of weakness, and I had tried to follow this. But on the stage I found release. The only other future which attracted me was an academic one.

I became more and more absorbed in the history of Ireland, but came across many paradoxes. The mythology of Ireland was essentially one of success: the ancient Celts lived under the Brehon law, a system of government on a clan system, with the kings of the clans not hereditary leaders but chosen by their followers. With the Norman invasion of Ireland the pattern changed to one of failure, with growing domination by the British and the British economic system. All Ireland's heroes were martyrs who had died for a cause: the one constant was defeat.

When we came to the twentieth century, we learned of the glorious rising of 1916, which had ended in the execution of its leaders. In their deaths, we were told, they had won freedom for the Irish people. Violence was the ideal, and death was the ultimate sacrifice. Strangely, the lessons stopped at 1921; we did not learn about the Civil War of 1922 and 1923, fought on the issue of whether Ireland should sign the treaty Britain offered, which accepted the partition of Ireland. Here the paradoxes were too intense. The Civil War had been won by the faction which accepted the treaty; this faction was opposed by Fianna Fail, which stayed out of the new Dail—Parliament— until 1927. But then, for thirty years Fianna Fail governed Ireland almost without a break. How could it govern a divided country when its founders had fought and died to try to prevent Ireland from accepting partition?

And then came more doubts. What was this freedom that Ireland's heroes had died to attain, the freedom proclaimed every year at the orations to the dead of 1916, the freedom enshrined in the country's first name: the Irish Free State (altered in 1949 to the Republic of Ireland)? I realized that Ireland remained totally dominated by Britain, with the system still existing by which Britain dominated Ireland in the nineteenth century. All Ireland had were symbols of freedom: our own flag, our own stamps, and our own sterling currency, which cannot be used in Britain, even though British sterling can be used in Ireland.

The "special position" of the Catholic Church had been guaranteed in the Twenty-six Counties by the 1937 Constitution. This meant that there was no freedom in such matters as divorce and contraception; there was censorship; and education was effectively controlled by the Catholic Church. How could this be freedom? Was this what the martyrs of 1916 had died for? The Irish government's claims to be free were totally hypocritical: Ireland was neither free nor independent nor a Republic. The only way to freedom was to develop independently in an economic sense, yet Ireland had never done that. It was a fine thing to have heroes who had died gloriously for freedom, but their deaths had achieved nothing, except to instill in other people the ideal that you should die for a cause, however vainly or hopelessly.

These were the thoughts preoccupying me in 1965, when I left school to start a course in English language and literature at University College, Dublin. This was Dublin's Catholic university; the other was Trinity College, which occupied a huge area in the very centre of Dublin, and to which the Catholic Church had been very hostile. It was only for Protestants, atheists, and Englishmen, and you had to ask your local bishop for permission to go there. Few Catholics did. Only the middle classes could send their children to University College, Dublin, as all education had to be paid for then, and working-class parents could not afford the fees. A degree was the path to success within the system, and there was little questioning of the basis of the system itself.

I enjoyed the course, which was very broad, encompassing European influences, and I was drawn to the tragedies of Shakespeare, the metaphysical certainties of Donne, the existential paradoxes of Camus. Of Irish writers I liked the romanticism of Yeats's poetry and identified with the intellectual struggles of James Joyce. But the rest of university life depressed me intensely. I had expected it would be the intellectual experience of my life. But the long discusssions among my fellow students were academic, theoretical, and parochial. The only issues of politics lay in the marginal differences between the two main political parties, Fianna Fail and Fine Gael; and even where dissatisfactions were voiced, no one contemplated ever doing anything to remedy them. No one talked about the IRA, and I knew of it only as figures from the past who wore trench coats and carried Thompson sub-machine guns. I knew nothing of the IRA's campaign in the Six Counties from 1957 to 1962, and the single event that impinged upon our consciousness was an explosion in March 1966 which wrecked Nelson's Pillar, a column erected by the British in O'Connell Street.

I was to take my finals in 1968. I had started acting at Dublin's Abbey Theatre and had been tentatively offered a place in the theatre company, but I decided to give up acting for six months to concentrate on the examinations. It was in this period that the civil rights movement began to show itself in the Six Counties. The demands were strictly reformist, for change within the system and within the boundaries of the Six Counties, asking for equality for the 500,000 Catholics of the North in jobs, voting, and housing. There was strong support for the Civil Rights Association in the Twenty-six Counties, but I felt uneasy at the Civil Rights leaders. They seemed too like the people I knew at university—convincing reasoners but ineffectual, the voice not, as they claimed, of the Catholic minority, but of an articulate few. As I saw it, the course they were taking was bound to lead them to a direct confrontation with the system. Preaching reform, they were bound to find themselves in a revolutionary situation, facing armed troops and unable to defend themselves.

I had come to hate Ireland, for the hypocrisy of its leaders, who pretended the country was free when it was tied in every way to Britain, and for the servility of its people, who accepted what the politicians told them, even though many of them knew it was untrue. I wanted the Irish people to be free, but they never could be so long as they had this slave mentality. I hated the oppression of the system in Ireland and the totalitarian position of the Catholic Church, which forced its views on me. The feeling of claustrophobia, of being imprisoned, built up in me until, ten days before I was due to take my final exams, I took all the sleeping pills I could find in our house and slashed my wrist. My mother found me on the bathroom floor, and I was rushed into hospital, and given a stomach pump and a blood transfusion. I left hospital the day before the examinations, took them, and passed. I also thought about why I had tried to kill myself, and decided that the only solution for me was to leave Ireland. I waited until the graduation ceremony to please my parents—I wasn't interested in the piece of paper I would be handed—and then went to Spain.

Spain to me was just a place on the map. It didn't matter to me that it was a Catholic, totalitarian country: all that mattered was that it wasn't Ireland. It was an advantage to me that I could not speak Spanish, because I knew I would be able to occupy my mind by learning it. I had no friends there—I would be completely cut off and would be able to begin again. My first base was Seville, and I travelled over much of the south; teaching jobs were well paid, but I did any work that came along, such as working in a bar.

Later I moved to Madrid and made friends among the Americans and Spanish and British people living and working there. I married an Englishman, but our relationship was disastrous and consequently short-lived. I also began a diploma course in psychology at Madrid University. Events in Ireland received considerable coverage in the newspapers and on Spanish television, and I had been naturally interested in the emergence of the IRA when real violence flared in the Six Counties in 1969. The reform movement had provoked the Stormont government into strongly repressive action by the police, the Royal Ulster Constabulary (CRUC) and its Protestant auxiliaries, the B Specials, and there was serious rioting in Belfast and Derry. The British Army, in turn, had gone in, at first, it was claimed, to protect the Catholic population; but gradually the British were becoming the defenders of Stormont supremacy. Then I had learned of the appearance of the IRA in the conflict: the group attracting most attention was known as the Provisionals (I knew nothing then of the split by the IRA into two groups, the Provisionals and the Officials).

The Provisionals, I learned, had taken up arms to protect the Catholic population—but, more than that, they stood for a new

Ireland, free of British dominance. It was clear that they were prepared to work for this end by use of force. History showed that British control had never been overthrown against its will other than by the use of force. The British maintained themselves in power by force; the struggles for freedom in Aden and Cyprus showed that force could end their power. I was prepared to agree with the selective use of force in order to achieve a better system of government. The Provisionals were aiming to free not only the Six Counties but the Twenty-six as well: their goal was a new Ireland without either Stormont, the seat of government in the North, or Leinster House, in the South. And I believed that because of the actions of the British government in defending the Stormont system in the North, the conditions were present in which the Provisionals could carry through their plans. In July 1971 I decided to return to Ireland.

# 2

# Commitment to a Cause

*. . . I wanted to do something
for the movement immediately.*

My decision to return was very sudden, even though my thoughts had been turning to Ireland more and more. I belonged to an amateur repertory company in Madrid, most of whose members were British exiles; they spent their time discussing the latest affair someone else's wife was having, and drinking. We had been rehearsing Sheridan's *The School for Scandal,* which could not have been more appropriate. We were to put on two performances, in the theatre of an English school in Madrid, over a weekend. It was after the Saturday-night performance that I decided to leave. I booked my flight on Sunday, played Lady Teazle and went to a party that night, and caught the Dublin plane on Monday morning.

My parents were pleased to see me, as always when I returned; my mother was certain that I could not have been happy in Spain, away from the family. Almost my first questions to them were about the Provisional IRA. Who were they, and how could I join? My parents didn't know, and if they were surprised at my interest they didn't show it. Perhaps the IRA was so remote from their own experience that they could not imagine that I would actually become involved with them.

At that time the Provisionals were enjoying good publicity, and they were favourably reported in the press. The question of civilian casualties was not then a large one—this was before any of the bad incidents in which civilians were killed—and the Belfast Provisionals had just carried out a spectacular rescue from the Royal Victoria Hospital, the city's main casualty hospital. Four volunteers, dressed in white coats, had pushed an injured Provisional who had been under guard by British soldiers out of the hospital on a trolley. The rescue, which made the British look foolish, appealed to the romantic tradition of Irish politics; so long as the Provisionals carried out daring operations like these and were not involved in indiscriminate violence, they were bound to remain popular in the Twenty-six Counties. But my family knew little more about their activities than this kind of escapade. Nor did they realize that there were close connections between the present-day Sinn Fein and the IRA.

When I discovered that this was so, I looked up Sinn Fein in the green-and-yellow Dublin telephone directory and found an address, Gardiner Place, on the north side of Dublin. I did not know then of the split that had taken place in the IRA in 1969, and that there were now two factions conducting operations against the British. Gardiner Place was the headquarters of the "Officials": the Provisionals, to whom I had been originally attracted, had their office in Kevin Street, on the south side.

One evening, not knowing any of this, I went to Gardiner Place. The office was up some narrow stairs; there was a meeting in progress, and most of the dozen or so benches—some consisting of old bus seats—were filled by people around my age. But when I sat down I soon realized that this organization —I had by now heard the word "Official," but still did not appreciate its significance—was not for me. The discussion was of world revolution, and I was interested in revolution in Ireland; I also had the impression that the people there thought they could achieve revolution without using force. When I asked a question about the Six Counties, I was told that I had to look at the struggle there in the larger context of the world socialist revolution. I could see that the meeting was heading for a long, analytical discussion on the theory of revolution and it reminded me only too clearly of university, where people talked and talked and never achieved anything. I left.

For a time I was at a loss, but then one Friday night I tuned the television in to RTE, the Irish broadcasting system. A current-affairs programme was being shown, and there was a discussion about the North. One man was expressing ideas that were exactly in line with my own. He argued for the use of force; he talked not of reform but of revolution, and not just in the Six Counties but in all thirty-two; and he presented his case logically, clearly, and without emotion. I learned that his name was Sean O Bradaigh; and he was described as Director of Publicity for Sinn Fein, Kevin Street (the Irish press and television always shied away from referring to the "Officials" and "Provisionals" and used a more neutral geographical term instead). I knew that he was the man for me.

I panicked at the thought of not being able to make contact with him, so I telephoned the RTE studios in the Dublin suburb of Donnybrook and left a message asking him to call back. When he did I told him at once that I wanted to join the Provisionals. He was undoubtedly surprised and asked me why. I told him, but he seemed more interested in my background than in my reasons.

He called to see me the following afternoon, at my parents' house, and brought me some literature about the movement's social and economic programme, about Sinn Fein's background, and about the split with the Officials in 1969. I told him that I already knew the aims of the movement. Again he asked me questions about my background. I discovered later that he took such an interest in it, and came personally to see me so quickly, because the Provisionals were trying to broaden their support, extending it among people such as myself who were not Republican by tradition. Quite soon afterwards Sean sent along a reporter from the London *Observer,* Colin Smith, to interview me as an example of the new type of middle-class member the movement was attracting.

I told Sean I wanted to do something for the movement immediately. He said that he was on his way to a Sinn Fein meeting at the country town of Mullingar, fifty miles northwest of Dublin; would I like to go with him? We drove there in his car and discussed the aims of the movement. I was very relieved that I had found someone with whom I could discuss my own ideas, and I was delighted to be able to do so dispassionately. I had always distrusted the use of emotion in political argument, and Sean didn't deploy the usual crude rhetoric about the heroes of 1916 and how the Irish should kick the British out. He put forward a constructive programme to break British military and economic control, to abolish both Stormont in the Six Counties and Leinster House in the Twenty-six, and replace them with a new system of government embracing all thirty-two counties.

My first Republican meeting could have killed my interest forever. It was held in the open air in Mullingar's main square to attract the Saturday-afternoon crowds. There was a truck draped with a tattered Irish tricolour in the middle of the square. Paddy Kennedy, the Republican Labour MP at Stormont for Belfast Central, one of the city's Catholic areas, was due to speak, but he didn't turn up. Most of the local Republicans who spoke shouted the customary slogans about the British; but Sean spoke forcefully and lucidly, and that held my interest.

We went for tea afterwards to Mullingar's small main hotel and sat with the local members of the Republican movement. Everyone seemed to be related and spent most of the time discussing each other's birthdays and illnesses. The week's main scandal was a meeting the local Young Socialists had held. It had developed into an "orgy," my companions complained, even though all that seemed to have happened was that one or two Young Socialists had got drunk. I could recognize the narrow-minded Irish mentality, which had been one of the chief reasons why I had left Ireland in the first place.

But despite these reservations, I was sure that, with just a few people like Sean O Bradaigh to steer it, the movement could be maintained. I told Sean in the car as we headed back to Dublin that I wanted to carry on. Sean kept in contact with me almost daily after the meeting at Mullingar, telephoning me or calling round to discuss documents he was preparing on social and economic policy. He seemed to value my opinions as those of a comparative outsider; perhaps it was surprising that he should have involved me in policy matters so quickly, but I soon found that the group of people with whom he could discuss such things was very small and that any additional member was welcomed, to help spread the work load. Quite soon afterwards I began to help write scripts and prepare tapes for a private radio project the Provisionals were hoping to set up, with stations both in the Six Counties and in the Twenty-six.

Then Sean sent me to a Sinn Fein Cumann, a district meeting of the Sinn Fein party. It was to be held in the office in Kevin Street, which was maintained and run in the name of Sinn Fein, legal in the Twenty-six Counties, though not in the Six. The office was used as well by the leading members of the Provisional IRA, which was illegal in both the Six and the Twenty-six Counties. When I arrived at 2A Kevin Street I could find only a shop called Home Knitters Ltd. I asked several passers-by, but they couldn't help me; then I discovered a small name plate by a tiny door which opened onto a flight of concrete stairs.

The meeting was like an episode from *Alice*. Everyone sat round in huddles, nobody asked me who I was, and I didn't even realize when the meeting had begun. Fortunately Sean rescued me. He telephoned to say that he had a job for me: there was more work to be done on the tapes for the pirate radio.

The principal event everyone was discussing in my first weeks in the movement was the shooting by the British Army of two Catholics in the city of Derry, eighty miles northwest of Belfast. (The British and the Unionists always called it Londonderry—"London" was added by the British Protestant merchants who arrived there to colonize Ireland in the seventeenth century. The name you used—Derry or Londonderry—at once indicated your allegiances; I remember how Heath always accentuated "London" so strongly that the "Derry" part was almost lost—"Londondre." Other terms were equally revealing: "Northern Ireland" (British and Unionist) or "Six Counties" (Catholic and Republican); likewise "Irish Republic" or the "Twenty-six Counties").

The first Catholic who was shot was Seamus Cusack, unemployed, like 25 per cent of the city's Catholic population. The British said he was carrying a rifle, but he was not even a Republican. The next day, in the rioting that followed Cusack's death, the second man was shot: Desmond Beattie, aged nineteen, also unemployed. The British once again suggested that he was throwing a gasoline bomb, but all the eyewitnesses said this was untrue. There had of course been other shootings of civilians in the Six Counties; but the particular bitterness these deaths caused led to six Stormont MPs for Catholic areas in the Six Counties, who had formed themselves into an alliance called the Social Democratic Labour Party (SDLP), walking out of Stormont and refusing to take part in its proceedings again. The SDLP spent much of its energy trying to hold the support of the Catholic population in the face of rivalry from both the Official and Provisional IRA, and its walk-out had been motivated partly by a fear of not appearing to act decisively enough.

The shootings, though, formed part of the escalating war in the Six Counties; the Provisionals, far more active than the Officials, were exploding on average two bombs a day, with sudden bursts of activity rising to twenty bombs a day. Both Provisionals and Officials were hitting at the British Army, which lost four soldiers killed and nearly thirty injured from April to August. This was the climate in which came the first major political event to occur after I had joined the movement, and one of the milestones in the history of the present Irish struggle: internment.

Internment had been argued for loud and long by the Stormont Unionists, and in particular Brian Faulkner, who had been Prime Minister of Northern Ireland since March. Eventually the British agreed; and on August 9 the British Army swooped. By that night it had arrested 342 people and held them, without charging them, under the Northern Ireland Special Powers Act, which had been used against Republicans in the Six Counties since 1922.

It was my mother who told me the British had begun internment. I was in bed, and she woke me that Monday morning with the news. Sean had told me that internment was coming —although we did not know the exact date—but I still felt angry. It was a day of great confusion, with reports coming through of who had been picked up and who had escaped. Then gradually it became clear that the Provisionals' command structure in the Six Counties had been left largely intact. The British had picked up many of the Officials, who had always been articulate and prominent in attacking British power in the Six Counties; and they also knew of the old-guard Republicans who had taken part in the previous largely abortive IRA campaigns of the 1940s and 1950s. But many of the Provisionals were soldiers at street level, who had joined the movement to defend themselves after 1969, and here the British intelligence was obviously quite sparse.

The British also picked up Civil Rights activists and other figures who were popular in the Catholic population, even though they might have actively and publicly opposed the use of force. The anger that these arrests in particular caused was of great help to the Provisionals. The British could have thought of no more effective way of helping to recruit members for the Republican movement if they had tried.

All that week, the Provisionals held meetings outside the Dublin post office in O'Connell Street, one of the most renowned locations of Irish Republican mythology: in 1916 the Irish rebels held the post office for a week against the British and proclaimed a new Irish government. Every night the crowds coming to our meetings were so huge that the street had to be closed to traffic. The speeches made from the back of a truck by members of the movement were very violent and emotional. I remember a tremendous roar greeting the facile statement "We don't want lollipops, we want guns." Internment would mark the year of Irish freedom; "We're going to end it for all time," proclaimed another speaker. Collections at the meetings brought in hundreds of pounds, with many one-pound or five-pound notes among the silver.

The campaign received a further boost from the news of a dramatic and cheeky press conference given in Belfast by Joe Cahill, until then leader of the Belfast brigade and one of the veterans of the movement. In 1942, during an earlier IRA campaign in the Six Counties, he had been one of six men sentenced to death for the killing of an RUC constable—the policeman was shot in a gun battle that typically had developed from a botched attempt to create a "diversion" while the IRA held a brief illegal Easter ceremony elsewhere. Five of the men, including Cahill, were reprieved; one, Tom Williams, commanding officer of the squad, who had not fired the fatal shot but nevertheless accepted responsibility, was hanged. Cahill spent seven and a half years in prison before he was released. Then in 1957, at the beginning of the IRA's next campaign, he was interned in Belfast's Crumlin Road jail under the same 1922 Special Powers Act that in August 1971 had just been used again. He spent a further four and a half years inside. He took part in the walk-out which led to the formation of the Provisionals in 1969, and in March 1971 became leader of the Belfast Provisionals, when the Belfast commander, Billy McKee, was arrested. As such, Joe naturally headed the list of Provisionals the British wanted to pick up. But he escaped the swoop of August 9 and four days later held a press conference in Saint Peter's secondary school in the strong Catholic area of Ballymurphy. That day the British Army's Northern Ireland chief of staff, Brigadier Marston Tickell, had claimed that the army had inflicted a "major defeat" on the IRA. Joe replied that they had lost only thirty men interned—and the very fact that he could give a press conference underlined how far the Provisionals still controlled events. The press conference ended abruptly with the news that a large British patrol had entered the area, but the point had been made.

In Dublin, Joe's defiant gesture was hailed as a triumph for the Provisionals and an outrageous blow against the British. But it did mean that Joe's cover was well and truly blown, and he now had to retreat to Dublin for good. His place at the head of the Belfast brigade was taken by Seamus Twomey, another of the men who had stayed with Mac Stiofain at the time of the 1969 split. Joe naturally appeared at several of the anti-internment meetings in Dublin and was received as a hero.

It was at one of these meetings that I first met Ruairi O Bradaigh, Sean O Bradaigh's brother and the president of Sinn Fein. He was the only leading member of the movement I had heard of when I returned from Spain and made my first inquiries. He had been the IRA's chief of staff at the end of the IRA's previous campaign from 1957 to 1962, and as such had made the announcement ending operations in February 1962. He had been interned by the Twenty-six Counties government in 1957 and held in an internment camp at the Curragh, an army base beside a racecourse thirty miles out of Dublin. He had been the first of the Republicans interned during that campaign to escape from the Curragh, and did so with another of the Provisionals' present leaders, David O'Connell, whom I was also to meet that week. For weeks in the summer of 1958 they had watched the Irish soldiers cutting grass around the camp, leaving the cuttings piled up around the perimeter wire. Despite an edict from the IRA leaders in the Curragh that no escapes were to be attempted, they formulated a plan. They waited until the day of a camp football match and used the diversion it provided to hide in the grass by the wire. They waited until nightfall and then broke out. They were in danger from the full moon, so they linked arms to look like a courting couple and walked slowly away from the camp to a point on the road where a car was waiting for them. Soon after their escape O Bradaigh was appointed chief of staff and Dave O'Connell director of operations, to replace the imprisoned IRA leaders. The two of them eluded the Irish police until the end of the campaign.

Ruairi's most renowned military action had been to lead a raid on the British Army camp at Arborfield in Berkshire, England, the twelve-man raiding party escaping with five tons of arms. Three of the men were arrested, and the arms were traced, but the success of the raid itself undoubtedly helped build his reputation in a movement accustomed to failure and defeat.

I found it hard to believe that this was the man Sean now introduced me to. His teeth protruded, his hair stood up spikily —he looked more like Bugs Bunny than anyone else—and he spent a great deal of his time chatting inconsequentially to people who came up to greet him. Surely the president of Sinn Fein had more things to do with his time, I thought. His public persona was more impressive: he was a powerful speaker who could move the crowd to anger or tears as he wished; after his speeches his main concern was to find a café where he could have a cup of tea and two or three slices of brown bread. He was very friendly towards me, saying, as his brother introduced us, "Oh yes, I've heard about you."

Quite soon after we met, Ruairi, like Sean, questioned me in detail about my background, my three years in Spain, and my reasons for wanting to join the Provisionals. I learned later that his curiosity had a serious purpose—was I a British agent? As I had arrived so suddenly, he was entitled to be suspicious. But I obviously satisfied him that my attitudes were genuine.

Later on that week I met Dave O'Connell; I had gone back to Sean's house in Glenageary with Sean and Ruairi when he arrived with the draft of a document he had been preparing on the movement's scheme for a system of regional government for the Thirty-two Counties. But the main topic of conversation was internment.

Internment in the Six Counties had clearly been sought by Faulkner and agreed to by the British government in order to smash the IRA—and, equally clearly, the IRA had to demonstrate that it had failed. The movement's military campaign had been to bomb economic targets and to kill British soldiers, and these activities were now stepped up. (The figures were to show with what effect: in the four months following internment thirty soldiers died, compared with four in the four months leading up to internment. August, the month of internment, was also the first month in which there were more than one hundred explosions in the Six Counties.) With internment, the British intended to establish their control over us and prove that they governed the Six Counties; our countermove demonstrated the reality: that we, not they, had this control.

Dave O'Connell—his friends all knew him as Dave, even though he signed his name Daithi—had been a schoolteacher in Donegal when the British brought in internment; now he had decided to give up his job and devote himself fully to the movement. I thought, as he discussed the military tactics with Ruairi and Sean, that he must be the Provisionals' chief of staff, such was his presence and the energy he generated. He had the ability to take a discussion by the scruff of its neck, summarize the arguments, and point the way forward. Aged thirty-three, he was tall but thin—Ruairi had an incipient potbelly—and his

*Sean Mac Stiofain,*
*Provisional Army Council*
*Chief of Staff*

**Photograph courtesy of**
**Central Press Photos**

*Ruairi O Bradaigh,*
*President*
*of Sinn Fein*

**Photograph by Topix,**
**courtesy of the**
**London Sunday Times**

most striking physical characteristic was his eyes, slanting and very blue. He was very relaxed and seemed in control of everything around him.

Within the movement, something of charisma attached to his name; he was the person more than any other I had heard people talking about. Like Ruairi, he had served his military apprenticeship. One knuckle was missing from his right hand, and he had a line of scars across his stomach, where seven bullets from a Sten gun burst almost finished his IRA career while he was on operations in the Six Counties during the campaign of 1957–1962. He had survived when he was not expected to and spent six years in Crumlin Road prison in Belfast. After he escaped from internment in the Curragh with Ruairi O Bradaigh, he became the IRA's director of operations at the age of twenty.

But his reputation depended as much on his intellectual prowess as on his military achievements. (He was not, as I later discovered, the chief of staff, but he was a member of the Provisionals' ruling Army Council.) In 1969, when the Provisionals split from the Officials and the positions in the new movement were being filled, it was decided that he should act between Ruairi O Bradaigh, who was to concentrate on political questions, and Sean Mac Stiofain, the Provisionals' Chief of Staff, whose interests were primarily military.

From military matters at Sean's house that evening the discussion turned to how best the movement could take political advantage of internment. As a result of our meetings a large number of people had been calling in at the Kevin Street office and asking if they could join the movement—some said they wanted to join Sinn Fein, others "the IRA." We always asked them to fill out a form applying to join Sinn Fein, and it would be only if they had any particular military capabilities or experience that they would be put in touch with a Provisional military expert. For most of the recruiting for the Provisionals took place in the Six Counties, where the local commanders would welcome men from their own district, who knew the ground they would be fighting on, essential in an urban guerrilla situation. It wasn't possible to transplant people from the Twenty-six Counties into the struggle, especially as local officers would be reluctant to accept people they didn't know and trust.

So we were most anxious to involve new members in the political struggle, and Dave thought it vital to build an organization with a political base that would hold it together through the fluctuations of attitude towards the movement that were bound to occur. There was clearly a tremendous emotional wave in our favour at the time of internment, but Dave and Ruairi accepted that as the weeks passed this wave would recede until the next major issue arose. They knew that the military situation in the Six Counties would vary too; that there were bound to be disappointments and setbacks. For many of the volunteers joining the Provisionals, the basic task was to defend their house or their street. They were unable to see the struggle even in the context of change in the Six Counties, let alone in the Thirty-two Counties of all Ireland. But a unifying political ideology would keep the volunteers' allegiance and hold the movement together.

# 3

# Provisional
# Politics

*There were so many targets
—banks, shops, cinemas, hotels.*

The need that Dave and Ruairi felt to develop the movement
politically had led to a decision to hold a convention at the end
of August to develop the whole concept of regional government. The Provisionals had been criticized for offering "no alternative" to the present system; here was its answer. The
movement's goal was a democratic socialist republic, and the
first step towards this would be to establish a system of regional
governments, one of them for the nine counties of the old province of Ulster, to be called the Dail Uladh. When the British
drew the borders of "Northern Ireland" they included only six
of those nine counties; even so, the British often call their state
"Ulster." The Protestants would still govern there, but with a
much slimmer majority. (In Stormont they always had at least
two-thirds of the fifty seats.) And the great advantage of discussing a nine-county Ulster was that it would open up the
issue of the border. The convention was to be held on August
21 in the Westenra Arms Hotel in Monaghan Town. We invited people from all political groups—we certainly didn't in-

tend to appear an exclusively IRA function—and among the politicians who agreed to come were Paddy Kennedy and Frank McManus, an MP at Westminster for Fermanagh and South Tyrone. (Voters in the Six Counties elected MPs to both Stormont in Belfast and the House of Commons in Westminster.)

Monaghan is a small Irish country town with just one thing to recommend it to us: it was close to the border and therefore accessible to people and groups wanting to come to the convention from the Six Counties. The convention was well attended, with a large press corps from many European countries as well as the British and Irish newspapers. There seemed to be genuine interest from groups outside the IRA in the possibilities of our idea; a committee was chosen to develop the idea further, with Paddy Kennedy as chairman, Frank McManus vice-chairman, and Dave O'Connell treasurer.

After the convention Dave took me to see a stone memorial that had been erected in Monaghan the year before to Fergal O'Hanlon, one of two IRA men who died in the raid in which Dave took part on the Royal Ulster Constabulary barracks in the Six Counties town of Brookeborough, County Fermanagh, in January 1957. But the raid—of which he now told me the story—ended in débâcle and retreat, with O'Hanlan and another man, Sean South, seriously wounded. The party reached a cowshed, by which time O'Hanlan and South were both unconscious; Dave was involved in the decision to leave them in the shed as the rest continued their flight. Dave and the other survivors escaped into the Twenty-six Counties, where they were picked up and sentenced to six months under the 1939 Offences Against the State Act for refusing to answer questions. But the question whether the RUC had finished off O'Hanlan and South when they reached the cowshed, or whether O'Hanlan and South had died already, still preoccupied Dave in 1972. He knew that they had had no alternative but to leave South and O'Hanlan, who was a close friend of his, but he had not been able to rid himself of the thought of the two wounded men dying by RUC bullets. South had quickly been immortalized in the rebel song "Garry Owen."

The convention at Monaghan was the first of two overt political moves the Provisionals made in the aftermath of internment: the second was the drawing up by the Army Council of the "Five Points," in which it stated its negotiating position for the ending of hostilities in the Six Counties. The Provisionals were already looking ahead to the possibility of a truce with the British; they knew that internment had failed to halt their campaign—it had in fact given it new impetus; and they knew that even if the British government didn't know it then, it would eventually come to do so. The Provisionals therefore had to state their demands so that the British government knew where they stood.

Dave had hoped that I would be able to take the statement containing the five points to London and hand them in to 10 Downing Street, naturally thinking of the publicity that would result from this. But I was in the middle of a short stay in Dublin's Mount Carmel hospital, having treatment for stomach ulcers; I left the hospital for an afternoon to meet Dave and Ruairi in the Russell Hotel to go through the wording of the statement with them. On September 4 Dave telephoned the statement through to the news agencies, the three Dublin daily newspapers, RTE, and the BBC.

There was a strong reason why Dave could not have waited until I left hospital a day or so later. On September 5 the Twenty-six Counties' Prime Minister, Jack Lynch, was due to meet Edward Heath at Chequers for talks on the Irish "problem." We knew that this would be a charade and that nothing meaningful in our terms would result. Lynch himself was naturally opposed to the new system of government we were fighting for and was not even interested in the united Ireland he said was inevitable. Why should the South want one million dissident Protestants, or a bankrupt Six Counties which was only surviving on the hundreds of millions of pounds the British poured into it? There was not even any influence Lynch could bring to bear on the British. As his party, Fianna Fail, itself pointed out, two-thirds of the Twenty-six Counties' exports went to Britain—which comprised only 5 per cent of Britain's total imports.

But by releasing our statement the day before his meeting with Heath, we knew we would be able to ride the publicity the Chequers talks would receive. We also considered it vital that other people should always appear to react to us, and not vice versa. If our statement had appeared *after* the Lynch-Heath meeting, it would have seemed that we were simply following lamely behind.

The statement began with a plea to Edward Heath to end "the agony of our people." This could be done, we proposed, if the British government would agree to do five things:

1 /End its campaign of violence against the Irish people.
2 /Abolish Stormont.
3 /Hold free elections to establish a regional parliament for the Province of Ulster as a first step towards a new government for the Thirty-two Counties.
4 /Release all Irish political prisoners, tried or untried, in England and Ireland.
5 /Compensate all those who had suffered as a result of British violence.

If the five points were accepted by September 9, we said, the Provisionals would suspend all operations. But if they were ignored, the Provisionals would intensify their campaign.

The proposals were dismissed out of hand by press and politicians alike: a contemptuous Stormont spokesman was quoted as saying that as they came from the Provisionals they could not even be discussed. But we held this to be an important first step in setting forth our political position and in establishing ourselves as a body which could not be ignored when it came to considering the future of Ireland.

But not everyone agreed with Dave and Ruairi on the importance of the political campaign; and the man to whom it seemed to mean least of all was Sean Mac Stiofain, the chief of staff of the Provisional Army Council. Mac Stiofain had been chief of staff of the Provisionals since the split with the Officials in 1969. The reasons for the split were complex and as concerned with personalities as with policies. But the principal points of disagreement were over the Officials' attitude towards military action and the kind of Ireland they wished to see in the future. The Officials, said the Provisionals, were not prepared to go on the offensive against the British Army, and their politics were altogether too Marxist. "They're all Communists," I was told on several occasions—a statement which I recognized as stemming as much from the Catholic beliefs of many Provisionals as from any deep political analysis. My own feeling about the Officials was that they were very good at talking, explaining, arguing, and justifying; but strangely hesitant when it came to actually doing anything.

There had been a great deal of bitterness after the split, and for some time both Dave O'Connell and Ruairi O Bradaigh carried revolvers and kept arms at their homes, despite the risk of being picked up and charged for possessing weapons by the Irish Special Branch. Dave himself had been the first to use the term "Provisional": the break-away group would set up an army council that would remain "provisional" until the divisions between the two factions were resolved—which of course in three years they were not. Later, most people referred to the Provisionals as Provos or Provies.

Ironically, Mac Stiofain's counterpart at the head of the Official IRA was Cathal Goulding, with whom Mac Stiofain had been sentenced to eight years in prison in England in the 1950s. They had taken part in a raid on the arms store of the cadet force of an English public school, Felsted, in Essex. Mac Stiofain then was known as John Stephenson, a railwayman from North London who had served in the RAF. The raid was another of the failures of the 1950s campaign: they had actually got away with a good haul of rifles and machine guns but as they headed for London were stopped by two police patrol cars who thought their van looked overloaded. Mac Stiofain had adopted his Irish name and learned the Irish language while in prison.

I first met Mac Stiofain in Monaghan; the first meeting of the committee set up by the convention of August 21 was due to be held there, although Mac Stiofain himself was in Monaghan to meet some of the active volunteers from our border units. He had a London accent that was even more pronounced when he talked in Irish, and I was suprised, as I had been with Ruairi, at how undistinguished he seemed; I was probably still cherishing romantic notions of IRA leaders as rugged heroes. He seemed short and squat and lacked Dave's physical presence: only later did I realize he was in fact over six feet tall. He appeared a little taken aback by me, too; I knew he had heard about me, but possibly he wasn't expecting someone wearing hot pants to be interested in the Provisional IRA. Someone said to me afterwards, "Maybe you'd be more acceptable if you had a limp and a squint."

I noticed a certain air of tension between Mac Stiofain and some of the other Provisionals leaders on the day of that first encounter: later Dave was to explain to me the differences over policies that were being felt and voiced on the Army Council. Mac Stiofain, Dave felt, was visibly bored by the arguments for the need of a political campaign, and paid only lip-service to the political activities Dave and Ruairi were trying to develop. Mac Stiofain had at first seen no point in communicating with the British at all, and Dave had to persuade him that the Five Points were worth while: indeed, he felt at first that to have any contact with the British was in itself a compromise, a betrayal; and he seemed to think that the movement's aims would be achieved by military means alone. At one point he agreed to attend the fortnightly meetings of the Ard Comhairle, the policy-making committee of Sinn Fein; but if he went at all he would find some excuse to leave—to make an essential telephone call, for example—and then not return. Dave certainly accepted the need for a military campaign and played a full part in developing its strategy and tactics; but it was always to be balanced by a political campaign that would keep the Provisionals at the centre of discussion about Ireland's future and give the movement a true basis for unity.

It was in early September, I learned later, that the first public move was made in the struggle for influence over the Provisional movement. At an Army Council meeting Dave proposed, quite simply, that Mac Stiofain should be replaced as chief of staff by Joe Cahill, the former Belfast commander who had come to Dublin after his dramatic press conference in Ballymurphy immediately following internment.

But for a man with such a declared interest in politics, Dave's attempt to depose Mac Stiofain was naïve in the extreme. The council then consisted of Mac Stiofain; Dave; Ruairi; Joe Cahill; J. B. O'Hagan, who had been on the IRA Army Council during the 1957–1962 campaign; Dennis McInerney, another veteran of 1957–1962; and Paddy Ryan, an explosives and training officer of strong but simplistic beliefs. Perhaps Dave had an idealistic belief in the possibilities of the democratic process, but he had lobbied none of the other council members beforehand, and Ruairi—as he later told me— knew from the surprised reactions on the others' faces that Dave's proposal was doomed. It is possible that, if he had prepared his ground beforehand, Dave could have succeeded; Mac Stiofain's own power base was not as secure then as it was later to become. But only Ruairi voted for Dave's proposal, and Mac Stiofain now knew precisely who his enemies were.

On August 25 the first really bad incident of the bombing campaign involving civilian casualties occurred. Volunteers placed a gelignite bomb in the computer room of the headquarters of the Electricity Board of Northern Ireland in South Belfast, but when a warning was telephoned to the switchboard the operator wouldn't take it seriously at first. "You're pulling my leg," she told the girl volunteer who called. "If you don't move fast you won't have any legs to pull," was the reply. When the Electricity Board authorities finally ordered the evacuation of the offices, it was too late: the bomb went off as many of the staff were going down the stairs, and one man was killed; about three dozen people were injured, including many girls. Two days later we issued a statement saying that Belfast had given "reasonable warning" and that the Provisionals "sincerely regretted" the casualties—and repeating that the only way to peace lay in a Thirty-two County Irish Republic based on the 1916 Declaration. The Army Council had decided to increase its bombing campaign following internment, and the Electricity Board incident illustrated the risks involved. Where there was the possibility of misunderstanding in the warning system, there was always the danger of civilian casualties. The Provisionals were, of course, accused of causing the casualties deliberately, but this was never the policy.

The intention behind the bombing campaign was to cause confusion and terror. In 1971 bomb explosions averaged three a day throughout the Six Counties, and it was very easy to cause confusion in the centre of Belfast. There were so many targets—banks, shops, cinemas, hotels. The British had to deploy large numbers of troops there, and this kept them out of the city's Catholic ghettos. It was an obvious guerrilla tactic, allowing our volunteers to move more freely and taking the heat off the Catholic population who were supporting them and giving them cover. Every bomb warning tied up hundreds of troops and police, even if it was only a false alarm. It was possible to cause widespread disruption of the city's life, with houses and offices evacuated, streets cordoned off, and buses rerouted. Sometimes the Belfast Provisionals would give a succession of false alarms and then, just as the city was enjoying the lull, plant half a dozen bombs on the same day. We believed that the bombing campaign had a greater psychological effect in this way. By causing such terror we demonstrated that, whatever steps the army took, the Provisionals could continue the military campaign; half a million people in Belfast would be kept wondering where the Provisionals would strike next and would be forced to tell the British to make peace with us. The terror we caused demonstrated that the British government could no longer govern. The campaign was aimed at economic targets such as the Electricity Board Headquarters. It was intended to bring life in the Six Counties to a halt, drive out international investors, and make it so costly for the British to repair the damage we were causing that they would have to meet our demands.

Accidents were accepted as an unfortunate by-product of the campaign and its intensification. When something did go wrong, the Army Council would always try to check it out by asking for a report from the local commander. In this case the Council did accept that the Electricity Board had been too slow and bureaucratic in dealing with the warning. I remember, though, that as we travelled through the Twenty-six Counties at meetings to present the regional government scheme, we were asked about this incident a number of times. It seemed a clear enough warning that civilian casualties would cost us support.

Then the headlines went to two other events. There was first an incident at Crossmaglen, a village close to the border in County Monaghan. Two British Ferret armoured cars had crossed into the Twenty-six Counties—inadvertently, said the British Army—but had been surrounded by local people and prevented from leaving long enough for local Provisionals to prepare an ambush. When the Ferrets did try to return they were fired upon, and an Army corporal was killed. All the argument turned on just where the ambush had taken place: in the Twenty-six Counties, said the British Army, which was upset at the notion of the IRA operating from within the sanctuary in the South; in the Six Counties, said both Lynch and ourselves, forming the most temporary of alliances—Lynch because he didn't want the British to lean on him to take action against us in Dublin; ourselves because we didn't want Lynch to have an excuse to do so either. We issued a statement congratulating the local Provisionals "who efficiently and speedily went into action against the enemy." The incident had been an isolated one for us, but by the end of the year the Army Council, having given serious thought to the possibilities of border action, had begun a concerted campaign.

The second incident was of benefit to us and also altered the attitude of some of the leading Provisionals towards publicity in the press and on television. In 1970 Dave O'Connell had visited the United States on a fund-raising tour—one of the main ways we raised money, especially from the fervent Irish-American communities of the East Coast. Now it was decided that Joe Cahill, a public figure since his Belfast press conference, should make such a tour. But the scheme met with an instant hitch when Joe was refused entry at Kennedy airport after the arrival of his Aer Lingus flight from Dublin. The reasons given were that his visa had been revoked and that he was a convicted person—referring to his part in the murder of a Belfast policeman in 1942. The British said coyly that they had "pointed this out" to the United States immigration officials, while denying that they had asked the Americans to keep Joe out. He spent eight days in the custody of the immigration officials and was photographed rather forlornly taking exercise behind wire netting on the roof of their offices. He had just time to declare, at an immigration hearing, "The British Army has raped our country," before being returned to Dublin. Even so, the publicity the case attracted helped the movement, and made Joe the most widely known of the Provisional leaders. Until then, the Provisionals had tended to operate more by stealth; now they saw the use that could be made of personal publicity.

# 4

# Gun-Running
# on the Continent

*"Maria is on an operation
. . . but don't worry."*

During my first two months in the movement I worked almost exclusively on the political side, helping both Sean and Ruairi O Bradaigh. (The pirate radio made one broadcast in Dublin and was then abandoned; it was supposed to have broadcast from Derry too, but never did so. The project had simply been beyond the movement's capabilities. Some Belfast battalions, however, did operate their own short-range pirate radios later. Andersonstown, for example, had Radio Saoirse.) Ruairi took an almost fatherly interest in me and was careful to keep in contact with me when Sean went on holiday, as if fearing that my enthusiasm for the movement might wane.

But then suddenly I became involved in the military side of the Provisionals' activities: a spectacular operation which put the Provisional IRA on the front pages of the world's newspapers, even though the operation ultimately failed. I was in Monaghan one afternoon late in September for another meeting of the regional government committee, when Dave O'Connell phoned and asked Ruairi to bring me back to Dublin that evening; he said he wanted to take a telephone call from my parents' house. (For some time the house was used for phone calls because it was believed to be unknown to the Special Branch.) We arranged to meet Dave that night at the Kilimanjaro, a cheap restaurant often used by the Army Council because it was one of the few places in Dublin where you could get a meal late at night. Afterwards Dave dropped Ruairi off, and then as we drove to my parents' house he asked me to go to the Continent with him.

I said I was quite prepared to; having joined the movement, I was ready to do anything for it. Dave said, "I perhaps ought to tell you it's to do with weapons." I had assumed this already. "I didn't think we were going to look at the sights," I told him.

The call, due at 11:30, was connected with the operation. It was from an American who called himself Freeman, who had come into the Kevin Street office several weeks earlier and said that he was able to supply arms. Dave had talked to him and then agreed to a deal with the Army Council. Freeman had left for the Continent to set the deal up and was now to phone to tell Dave with what success.

At that time, having been involved with the movement for only a matter of weeks, I did not know much of the background to the deal or why it was so important. But I was able to piece much of this together later, from what Dave told me while we were on the Continent, and from what I learnt from him and other members of the movement, such as Joe Cahill, during the rest of 1971 and the first half of 1972.

When the shooting war started in earnest in the Six Counties in 1969, the IRA had all but disarmed, only a few people having realized the possibilities presented by the Civil Rights campaign. In fact, so sure was the IRA leadership that it would take many years for the political phase to develop to the stage when arms would be needed that in 1968 it actually sold some of its precious weapons to the Free Wales Army, a tiny group of nationalists from Wales who were promptly arrested. Most

*David O'Connell,
member of the
Provisional Army Council*

**Photograph courtesy of
Syndication
International**

*Maria McGuire,
publicity officer of the
Provisional IRA*

**Photograph by
Jane Brown, courtesy of
*The Observer***

of the firearms in civilian hands in the Six Counties belonged to Protestants who were either B Specials, members of rifle clubs (often affiliated to the local B Company), or farmers—the majority of whom are also Protestants. There are plenty of stories, mostly apocryphal, of sixteen-year-olds with .22 rifles holding rioting Protestant mobs off from the working-class Catholic areas in Derry and Belfast when the dam finally burst in August 1969.

By the time I joined the Provisionals all this had changed. Reliable supply lines with Irish-Americans in the United States —the traditional source of arms for the Irish Republican movement—had been established, and weapons started to trickle in at a reasonable rate. But it *was* only a trickle, usually in the form of three or four weapons at a time, packed into false-bottomed cases in ordinary air and ship freight.

Most of these weapons were World War II military rifles, such as the M1 carbine, the heavy Garand semi-automatic rifle (it weighs twelve pounds), bolt-action Springfields, and British Lee-Enfields—thousands of which were sold to arms dealers in the United States as hunting rifles when the British Army went over to SLRs in the late 1950s. There were also a few .222 Magnum French hunting rifles that are good for short-range sniping at distances up to 200 yards.

The rest were assorted pistols of vastly differing types and calibres, plus a few sub-machine guns, mostly the famous Thompsons. Other people call them tommy guns, Chicago pianos (Al Capone celebrated Saint Valentine's Day with one), but most IRA men normally refer to them as "the Thompson," though some of the younger ones also called them "rattle-boxes." They do make an incredible din.

The gun was invented by an American colonel called Thompson in 1921, just in time for the Irish civil war. Hundreds of them appear to have been smuggled into the country at around that time, and they rapidly became as much a part of the IRA legend as the trench coat. The weapon holds a firm place in Irish folklore and is featured in several rebel songs: in "Dublin in the Green," for instance, where "the rifles crack and the bayonets flash to the echo of a Thompson gun." Many of the Irish Thompsons have spent more time under the ground than over it. Just after internment was introduced, I remember, a wizened old man came into Kevin Street and produced various parts of a rusty Thompson gun out of a brown paper parcel. " 'Tis a present from the boys in Cork," he announced. Many IRA men—Ruairi was one—will tell you that the Thompson is their favourite weapon.

But the attachment was more sentimental than practical. Northern Catholics who served in the British forces during the last war soon learned that the German Schmeisser and the British Sten gun were more than a match for the Thompson. One of the major faults with the Thompson is that, unless it's kept spotlessly clean (often difficult in combat conditions), it's prone to jamming; another is that it needs a strong man to handle it, because its barrel should trace an imaginary figure eight around the target; a third is that the Thompson has a relatively low velocity, and there have been instances in the North of its heavy .45 bullets failing to pierce soldiers' flak jackets. (High-velocity rifles go straight through them.)

Some United States army units were still using the Thompson in Korea, but nowadays it's strictly a collector's item. But as such it was easier to get hold of in the United States than contemporary sub-machine guns. Most of the .45 ammunition fired from Thompsons in the North is manufactured in Sweden.

Ammunition was a quartermaster's nightmare. Even when a steady flow of arms was coming in, we would never turn our noses up at a few extra rounds. A girl-friend of mine once robbed an ex-boy-friend, who used to go in for competition shooting, of a couple of hundred rounds. Much to Ruairi's horror, she came into Kevin Street and started plucking them out of her clothes. But the main problem was the different calibres needed for all the different weapons: .300 for the M1s and Garands; .303 for the Lee-Enfields (a good sniper's rifle, still used for countersniping by some of the British infantry regiments in the Six Counties); 7.62 for the odd SLR and FN we had got hold of; .45 for the Thompsons, and 9 mm. for the other sub-machine guns. Then on top of that there were all the various pistol ammunitions, from tiny .25 to .44 magnum.

Another snag was that bullets, even of the correct calibre, are far more individual in their behaviour than many people think. The performance of, say, the .303 rounds would vary enormously from batch to batch. This was particularly annoying for the really good snipers, who found that a shot that had worked out perfectly one day would fall short the next. (Of course the lads who just used to blaze away regardless didn't notice much difference.)

A large arms shipment of identical weapons and ammunition of recent manufacture—what Dave was aiming for on the Continent—would solve these problems. We could have equipped whole units with the same calibre weapons. We had also ordered several thousand rounds of ammunition made in Czechoslovakia to fit captured NATO 7.62 rifles. Dave was also after modern sub-machine guns to replace the Thompsons —and the Belfast Volunteers would certainly welcome the newer, more reliable weapons. Had the Czech arms arrived in the North we might well have forced the British to start thinking about a bilateral truce long before they did. As it was, the Belfast Provisionals had to wait almost another year before the World War II rifles were gradually replaced by Japanese AR 180 armalites—a super-high-velocity rifle that weighs only seven pounds and has a collapsible butt that allows it to be hidden in a packet of cornflakes.

The first large-scale attempt to smuggle in arms during the present campaign had been in March and April 1970, an attempt that was brought to light in the famous Dublin arms trial of September 1970. It was an astonishing and melodramatic affair involving the import of arms into Dublin airport from Vienna, and at one stage looked like bringing down the Lynch government, for there were clear allegations that several of Lynch's senior ministers had been involved. Lynch sacked two of them—one actually stood trial, but he was acquitted—and narrowly won a vote of confidence in the Dail. The affair was also the end of public activities for the movement for one of its leading members. John Kelly was a prominent member of the Belfast brigade (he had been imprisoned in the 1950s) who acted as negotiator for the Provisionals in the abortive deal. But he did so in the knowledge that if the affair came to light the Provisionals would have to disown him, and he would take the rap alone. Furthermore, it would be a crime in many Republicans' eyes to be publicly associated—as Kelly was at the trial—with members of the Fianna Fail parliamentary party, descendants of the men who sold out Republicanism by entering the Dail in 1927. The trial finished Kelly as an active volunteer in the Six Counties, and he was withdrawn to Dublin. The point is that the entire melodrama concerned a consignment of arms consisting of 500 pistols—principally defensive weapons, and of little use in a campaign against the British Army—and 180,000 rounds of ammunition. This in no way approached the quantity and importance of the arms Dave was now trying to bring in.

It was thus in a state of some apprehension that Dave now awaited the call from Freeman that would tell him how the deal was progressing. The call came through on time, and Dave seemed pleased at the outcome. Afterwards Dave said that he couldn't give me many details as yet; but he said he wanted me with him, because I spoke three languages fluently: French, German, and Spanish. He thought, too, that I was fairly cool, and that it would be easier for a girl to pass through customs controls with a large amount of money. Being with a girl would enable him to move around less conspicuously.

On Monday I met Dave in the Pirate's Den, a restaurant near the Intercontinental Hotel that we also used frequently.

The plan, Dave told me now, was that we should both fly to Paris from Cork the following day, taking £20,000 in banknotes with us. (Although I believe this was not the full amount we were to pay, I never found out what the total price would have been if the deal had been successful—and if this seems surprising, security considerations dictated that no one within the movement should know more about an operation than he needed to.)

But that night came the first of many hitches that were to bedevil the operation. The money had not yet come through. Much of our long-term fund-raising was done in the United States, but when a large amount of money was needed quickly and secretly it came from sympathizers in the Twenty-six Counties, businessmen who were not prepared to help us publicly but wanted to ease their consciences none the less. The asking was done by Joe Cahill, who worked closely with the movement's Dublin quartermaster, Jack McCabe, on such projects. Joe was asking for money at the right time, with emotions following internment still high.

But even so, that evening Joe telephoned to say that he had not yet managed to raise the money, although he expected it would come through shortly. And here the operation started to become insecure too: for to persuade the movement's sympathizers that the deal was worth-while he had to mention Dave O'Connell as the key man involved. Already the circle of people who knew something of the operation was beginning to widen.

When he heard Joe's news, Dave decided to go to Paris anyway to set the deal in motion. I would meet him in Zurich later that week, as soon as I had the money. I still knew few details of the operation but was sure by now that it was going to be very important to the movement that we succeed. In the rush, there had been no time to prepare false passports, and we would have to travel under our own names. That night Dave gave me a small flat grey American .38 automatic, which I slipped into my handbag. He had a similar weapon himself. In the morning he drove down to Cork and caught the plane to Paris, and I settled down—as far as I could—to wait to hear from Joe Cahill.

The first time Joe called he was obviously agitated: "Christ, it still hasn't come through," he said. "What the hell are they doing?" Dave rang that night and again the following evening, and was obviously worried by the delay; so, I presumed, was the arms dealer. Then some money arrived, but still only £10,000 which Joe brought up to my house in brown paper parcels. I kept them in my room. When Dave called on Thursday, we agreed I should fly to Zurich the next day with what I already had.

That night I tried to work out how I was going to carry all the money. The notes were mostly of small denomination. I had been given several canvas money-belts, into which I stuffed the notes. I pushed some into my leather boots and filled my handbag with the remainder. I felt like a penguin, as I tried to walk naturally, and wondered if I would ever be able to pass through customs unnoticed.

In the morning I went through the same performance and then put on a pullover belonging to my brother and a poncho over that. I went to Dublin airport to catch an early-morning plane to London, from where I would fly on to Zurich. It was an Aer Lingus flight, was predictably late, and I missed the Zurich connection. I spent five hours drinking coffee at Heathrow; the weather was very hot, I was sweating under all my clothes, and I made repeated visits to the ladies' lavatory to make sure the notes weren't falling out. I arrived in Zurich around six that evening. I walked through the customs so easily that I didn't even have time to feel nervous. But I was worried in case Dave was no longer waiting for me; if he had decided I wasn't coming that day, I would have no way of contacting him.

We had arranged that I should give a message, using a false name, over the airport's announcement system, but as I was walking to the desk I saw him coming towards me. He didn't stop but just muttered, "See you in the bar." I watched him going up the escalator and saw that two men, short and squat, with Slav features, appeared to be following him. He went into the restaurant, then moved on to the bar. When I met him there, he said, "I'm glad you're safe." He had been worried that I might have been arrested and he told me he wasn't sure whether the two men we had seen were following him or not. But they didn't seem to be with him any more.

We took a taxi to our Zurich hotel, large and old-fashioned. I was glad to divest myself of all the money, which lay all around the bathroom as I showered. After I had changed, we parcelled up the money and left it in the hotel safe in a room behind the reception desk. When we went for a drink, Dave told me he had been to Berne for a Czech visa. The arms, four and a half tons, were coming from the Czech Omnipol arms factory in Prague. He was sure he was being followed, probably by the Czech or Russian secret police.

That night we met the American Freeman, who had set the deal up. He was tall and broad, with short-cut blond hair, and glasses. Dave seemed very impressed by him, and they became friendly; but I didn't take to him at all.

Freeman wanted Dave to meet the arms dealer himself in Brussels the following night, Saturday. We arranged to meet Freeman at Brussels airport early on Saturday evening— although Freeman also gave us the name of the night club where the dealer would be waiting, in case our plane was delayed. Dave had already met the dealer once, in Paris, while I was still in Dublin waiting for the money to come through. He didn't like the dealer, he told me: he didn't trust him. Nor did he trust Freeman completely, he claimed, and decided not to tell Freeman that I would be coming to Brussels too. We arranged that I should try to follow Dave in Brussels, so that if anything went wrong I would at least know what had happened, even if I was powerless to do anything about it.

In Brussels we booked into the airport hotel, and Dave went to meet Freeman. I took a taxi to the street containing the night club where Dave and Freeman were to rendezvous with the dealer. I sat in a café almost opposite, ordered coffee after coffee, and waited. It appeared that we were in Brussels' red-light district, such as it was, and I spent much time staring icily ahead in order to dissuade the men who kept coming to sit at my table. After two hours Dave and Freeman emerged. I never saw the dealer at all. Dave went back to the hotel, and I followed him there.

Dave was obviously worried now, chain-smoking, drawing on his cigarette very quickly, and pacing from one side of the hotel room to the other. It had been arranged that he should go to Prague on Monday, but the deal was taking much longer than we had expected, and he was beginning to feel the strain. He also had the constant fear of the deal going wrong. Apart from the consequences for the movement itself, failure would seriously affect his standing within the Provisional leadership, giving Mac Stiofain the chance to strengthen his own position at Dave's expense. And if things did go wrong, how would the Irish people both inside and outside the movement react to the Provisionals making an arms deal with a Communist country?

We flew back to Zurich on Sunday, and in the afternoon Dave tried to relax. He drank a lot of Scotch, as he always did when he was trying to calm his nerves. That evening we both met Freeman again to make final arrangements for the journey to Prague. It was decided that I should fly back to Dublin to report on the progress of the deal and to collect the remaining £10,000.

Dave was to take the first £10,000 with him to Prague, where he had agreed to make a down payment, partly as a token of good faith, against delivery of the arms. Freeman had told Dave that the Czechs would want the money in Swiss currency—and it suddenly dawned on us that most of the notes we carried were Irish. Our hearts sank at the prospect of presenting our Irish money, knowing the consternation it caused anywhere east of Howth, with cashiers holding notes to the light and checking in endless ledgers that this Monopoly money was real. We were also afraid to change all £10,000 at once—a rather conspicuous transaction, we thought—so in the morning went from one bank to another, changing small amounts each time. Our fears were confirmed. At every bank there was confusion and suspicion, and the cashiers spent a long time scrutinizing the notes and checking and rechecking the exchange rate. Then between each visit I had to find a lavatory in which to put the Swiss money away and take out more Irish notes. As I look back, the whole performance was ludicrous and probably far more risky than if we had changed all the money at once. Certainly at the time I felt sure that every police force in the world knew what was going on. We could hardly have drawn more attention to ourselves.

We met Freeman briefly yet again at one—he said everything was OK—and then hurried to Zurich airport for my plane to Dublin. It was, of course, delayed. Dave was carrying some of the money in a money-belt, the rest in his briefcase. (Now that it was in large-denomination Swiss currency it was far less bulky than when I had brought it from Dublin.) We arranged that I should fly back from Dublin on Wednesday, if possible, and meet him in Amsterdam.

Back in Dublin on Monday evening, I telephoned Joe Cahill. He had expected me back on Sunday and hadn't known we would be going to Brussels. I reassured him briefly that the operation seemed to be going smoothly, and when he came up to my parents' house I told him everything that had happened. He said he would make sure I had the second amount of money the following day, Tuesday; I especially asked that it should be in British sterling. I was to go to a house on the north side of Dublin to collect it in the evening.

I went to the house as arranged—and the money, as I half expected, wasn't there. On Wednesday morning Dave telephoned from Switzerland, and I had to tell him I wouldn't be able to come, as the money wasn't ready. I optimistically said I would come on Friday, on a direct flight from Dublin to Amsterdam.

The money came through on Thursday, in two batches. I collected half from the house in North Dublin, and Joe brought the remainder up to my parents' house that evening. It was in British sterling—but mostly five-pound notes again. When I told Joe I couldn't carry it, he said he would arrange for it to be changed. In theory, my contacts with Joe and Ruairi O Bradaigh should have been minimal, but because of all the things that had gone wrong this had proved impossible—and all the time more and more people were learning that there was a big deal under way on the Continent.

The most blatant example of our crumbling security concerned the arrangements being made for storing the arms in Amsterdam and then shipping them from Rotterdam into the Six Counties, where they were destined for Derry. Joe had told me that he had arranged with a Cork businessman for a warehouse to be available for us in Amsterdam. This man, Joe explained, would probably fly out himself to Amsterdam on Friday. The Cork man telephoned me at home on Thursday evening—I thought it was a risk even to give my telephone number. He said he did have a problem, because it was his wedding anniversary on Friday and he couldn't tell his wife he was going away in connection with—I quickly cut into the conversation because I was sure he was going to say "arms deal" over the phone. But he was sure everything would be all right and added that if ever I wanted to leave a message I could do so with his secretary, because she was completely trustworthy. I shuddered.

On Friday morning at eight, Dave phoned again. The weather, he said, was improving—in fact, it was 0.5 degrees warmer in Amsterdam. This wasn't polite conversation; according to a pre-arranged code, he was asking me to bring another

£2500. I telephoned Joe Cahill and told him. "I'm not too sure
about that," Joe said. I said that Dave considered it essential to
have the extra money, and he said he would see what he could do.

Joe called back at eleven and said that the money would be
delivered to my parents' house before I left; I said that if it
didn't come by two-thirty I'd have to leave to catch my plane
without it, as Dave's contacts on the Continent were becoming
uneasy. Joe had also arranged for someone to change the
£10,000 I already had, and he was due at midday. At 1:15 I
had everything packed to leave, and had ordered a taxi for
2:30. The man who was to change the money arrived at 1:30
and returned with it at 2:15. I had a quarter of an hour to stuff
the money into money belts and put them on, the taxi arrived at
2:30, just as I finished. But there was still no sign of the extra
£2500. I waited until 2:35 and then decided to go.

I learned later of the drama that unfolded shortly after I left.
Ruairi O Bradaigh arrived at 2:45, sweating, in complete panic.
Normally a cautious, methodical person, he had driven himself
to a state of complete anxiety in his efforts to catch me before I
left. He arrived at the house and asked my mother, "Is Maria
here?" When he learned I had just left he virtually collapsed,
and my mother had to take him into the house and give him a
cup of tea—and some brown bread—to revive him.

Then, shortly afterwards, there was a telephone call; it was
the Cork businessman, and he too asked, "Is Maria there?"
When my mother told him that I had gone, he said, "That's terrible," and asked my mother to take a message for me. "I'm
afraid I can't go to that place," he dictated to her, "because of
my wife's anniversary, but everything is all right because I've a
friend in Holland who looks after warehouses." I had told my
mother I was going away for a few days to Cork or Kerry—to
convalesce from my ulcers, I intimated—and this message left
her totally perplexed. Ruairi, standing beside her by the telephone, heard the harsh Cork accent and guessed what the call
was about. "Maria is on an operation," he told my mother,

adding, a little uselessly, "but don't worry."

I knew nothing of this at the time; I didn't know what the Cork businessman looked like and had not made firm arrangements to meet him, so I did not know whether he was on my flight or not. In Amsterdam I went through the customs laden with money, again without problems. It was almost a relief, in fact, to get back to the Continent after the confusion and last-minute panics of Dublin. I met Dave, who hadn't been there for long. He had to meet Freeman again that evening and he dropped me at the small hotel he had booked into in old Amsterdam; "There's a present in the room," he said as he drove off: it turned out to be a bottle of whisky.

When Dave returned, he told me what had happened in Czechoslovakia. He showed me a glossy Omnipol catalogue, profusely illustrated. The arms, he said, were very, very good; he was clearly very exhilarated about them. He had asked for an extra £2500 because for the small amount extra he could improve the deal considerably.

In the end it was not disastrous that I had missed Ruairi so narrowly, for on Saturday I was followed out to Amsterdam by another helper. He was a middle-aged single man from Donegal who was to help us with the arrangements for shipping out the arms after we had bought them. On Saturday night Dave met Freeman again and learned from him that there had been more delays and that the consignment of arms would probably not now arrive until the end of the week. Freeman suggested it would be safest if we left Amsterdam for the time being. We told the shipping man, whom I shall call Tom, that he would do best to go back to Dublin to wait too—and we told him to contact Joe Cahill when he arrived there in order to bring the missing £2500 with him when he returned. Dave and I decided to hire a car—it was a Ford Escort—to tour southern Holland and maybe go into Germany. Away from Amsterdam we managed to relax a little, although it was impossible to forget the arms deal completely.

We drove back to Amsterdam on Wednesday and booked into the Euromotel. At Amsterdam airport we met the shipping man from Donegal; he was very excited at having brought the money through customs, but by now he was becoming a little paranoiac about the secrecy surrounding the deal. British secret-service agents had been watching him at Manchester, he said—he could tell them from the Shell uniforms they wore as they pretended to service the plane. He was quite out of his depth. That evening we took Tom round Amsterdam. He was amazed at the prostitutes sitting in the windows doing their knitting, and the pornographic magazines on display; "If the lads in my local pub could see me now," he said. He also said that if his part in the deal ever became known, it would make headlines in the *Donegal Democrat*. I liked Tom, and I was afraid for him in case he was picked up although my worry did stem partly from a fear that he would talk.

The failure of the Cork businessman to help us in the end was unimportant now, for Dave had made contact with a Dutchman who would provide a warehouse for us to store the arms in while Tom and we arranged for them to be shipped from Rotterdam. I did not inquire how the arms would come through the Dutch customs; I assumed that it involved bribing a key customs official. We now expected the arms to arrive on Friday or Saturday of that week.

On Thursday, Dave was once again in contact with Freeman. Freeman said everything was all right and that the arms were due on Friday night. We went to check out the warehouse, a low building on a farm in the country just outside Amsterdam. Otherwise all we could do was wait. The deal was to be completed at the point when the arms were loaded into the warehouse, and Dave was certainly worried about the possibility of a sell-out. If there was to be a double-cross, it would come then, and it would be easy enough for anyone to pull a gun on us. Dave phoned Dublin and discussed with Joe the possibility of sending another helper, heavily armed, to guard against this.

But they decided there wasn't time. We were becoming very weighed down by the days of waiting and wondering about the outcome of the operation.

On Friday morning, Freeman, Dave, and the arms dealer had a further meeting. There were no problems, said Freeman—but there could be another delay. If the arms didn't arrive on Friday night, they would come on Saturday. We went to dinner that night, drank quite a lot, and booked into the first hotel we came to, the Delphi.

When I woke on Saturday morning, I had a feeling that something was going to go wrong. It may have been a combination of the days of waiting and a hangover; it may have been premonition. I told Dave how I felt; he said nothing. He was due to meet Freeman and the dealer at eight that morning. I met Tom from Donegal at ten to tell him the arms were expected at any time, and he confirmed that there would be a boat waiting for the load at Rotterdam. At midday I met Dave in the lounge of the Hotel Apollo. I knew then that something had gone wrong. He was acting with studied coolness, and the colour of his eyes seemed to have lightened. Even when he told me the arms had arrived at Amsterdam airport I knew we were in trouble. For a few minutes we had a normal conversation, and he ordered coffee. Then he tossed a copy of the *Daily Telegraph* onto the table and said, "Have a look at this." There was a short news item about Dave. It said that David O'Connell, believed to be the Provisionals' chief of staff, was on the Continent on a quest to buy arms for the IRA. I was so taken aback that I laughed. We had come so close to completing a huge deal and had now been exposed by a single paragraph in a British newspaper. (We had always joked that the *Telegraph* was staffed by the British secret service anyway.) I was to regret my laugh later. All Dave said was, "I bet Mac won't like that 'chief of staff' bit."

# 5

# Another
# Glorious Failure

*. . . suddenly he blurted out,*
*"Are you a British agent?"*

I asked Dave if the arms had been discovered. He said he
didn't think so, but that Freeman and the arms dealer had
warned him that morning that there might be "trouble." He
hoped that the aircraft could be held at the airport for a day or
so while the trouble blew over, and then unloaded. Perhaps the
newspaper report was pure speculation—he wondered.

Then I noticed a man staring at us in the lounge. He was
tall, in his late twenties, with gold-framed spectacles and blond
hair. We came to know him as Mr. Apollo, not because he was
at all beautiful, but from the name of the hotel. Because he
made no attempt to conceal his interest in us, it seemed unlikely that he would be a policeman or security agent. Dave got
up to see if the man followed him, but he seemed to be concentrating on me. Then Mr. Apollo got up, walked towards the
window of the lounge, turned on his heel, walked towards me,
and stopped no more than a yard away. He stared at me hard,
and I looked at him blankly.

I knew then we were in trouble, but who was he? If he was

from the British police, the Dutch police, or the CIA, was he behaving in this obvious way because he was sure we were trapped? He unnerved us so much that we decided to lose him. We left the hotel and walked through the streets; when we finally looked back, he wasn't there.

The immediate problem was to decide what we were going to do—both about the arms and about ourselves. Dave phoned Freeman, who was by now very nervous about the whole deal. He said the heat was on, the *Telegraph* story had really worried him, and he advised us to leave Amsterdam; perhaps in a couple of days things would cool down and we could pick up the arms then.

But it seemed essential to discover just who was on to us. We went into another hotel in the same street as the Delphi, where we had spent the previous night. We had a transistor radio and listened to the BBC's *World at One* news programme: nothing. Then we decided that I should go back to the Delphi to see if Mr. Apollo—or anyone else—had been asking questions about us there. I went up to the reception desk and asked to change some English money into guilders.

It was obvious at once that the receptionist was anxious to confirm who I was. I had spent the night at the hotel, hadn't I? In room 311? Had the heating, the room service, the bathroom been to my satisfaction? The receptionist excused himself and went into a room at the back of the desk. I was sure he was telephoning the police. When he came back he tried to spin out the money-changing transaction as long as he could, but I just grabbed the money and hurried out. As I came out I heard the noise of a car engine, then saw a white police car coming up the road at speed. As I approached the Delphi it drew up outside the Apollo. Dave was waiting for me in the lounge. "They're on to us," I told him. From the lounge we could see two police cars now outside the Delphi. We couldn't leave until they had gone; there was still nothing on the news about us. We were determined not to leave Amsterdam if there was still a chance of getting the arms out of the airport. We decided to make for the narrow streets in the centre of Amsterdam, where we would be difficult to find; and we had an appointment that night with the Dutch warehouseman which we wanted to keep if we could.

At 7:30 we knew that the news had broken. We were going past a bar in the centre of the city, when I heard a news flash. I caught the words "arms" and "Schiphol airport." Then I saw pictures of opened crates full of weapons: four tons of them, said the news, had been discovered at the airport, and the police were looking for David O'Connell. I wasn't named. There was little we could do. We decided that we would still look for the Dutchman and in the meantime would stay where there were lots of people. We heard several further news flashes later that evening, developing the story. We were depressed at the knowledge that the deal was finished and that there could be no hope now of collecting the arms. But we were also preoccupied with the question of what to do. Whose names did the police have? Was I known? If I wasn't known, where should I go? Or would it be better to stay with Dave and provide him with some cover at least? And if I was known, would it be better to split up? And *who* was Mr. Apollo? Was he a British agent, we wondered, who would shoot us out of hand *pour encourager les autres?*

We had arranged to meet the Dutchman at the Victoria Hotel and arrived there shortly after 9:30. Once again, we didn't know if he would come now that the news had broken. He had said that he was quite prepared to store anything in his warehouse, so long as it wasn't drugs; he was being well paid, but I was sure he didn't realize that quite such a large consignment of arms would be involved. Dave hadn't even told him we were Irish. Just before ten, Dave went outside. He returned ten minutes later, having met the Dutchman, whom I shall call Jan. "Are you David O'Connell?" Jan had asked. When Dave said he was, Jan asked if he knew the police were looking for him.

Dave said yes, he did, and Jan asked if he had made any plans. Dave said he hadn't. Jan asked him if he wanted to use his house to hide in that night.

Dave, very taken aback by the generosity of this offer, accepted it. We were worried about the responsibility the Dutchman was taking on himself and his family and thought he could be in real danger, especially as we had no idea who was looking for us. But there was no alternative but to accept. Dave had arranged to meet him at the docks in half an hour, after we had dumped the Escort. We drove down to a railway station and stopped by the waterside on the opposite side of the road. We knew we had to get rid of every item of possibly incriminating evidence, so we took all our documents—arms catalogues, names and addresses—out of the car, and started tearing them up into small pieces and throwing them into the black water below.

We were naturally a little apprehensive as we carried out this operation, and, looking around me, I saw to my astonishment, some hundred yards away on the opposite side of the road, by a line of parked cars—Mr. Apollo. He watched us steadily, even impassively, as we threw our debris into the water. I thought to myself: "We're finished." What could we do? Nothing, it seemed, but continue what we were doing. It had to be done, and by now I was quite sure we were going to be arrested.

Then Jan arrived in his car. In full view of Mr. Apollo we got in and drove off. I was sure he could have taken the car number if he wanted to. But once again we had no alternative course of action. Who the man was, we never discovered. It is one of the many mysteries remaining in my mind about the entire operation.

We travelled to Jan's home on the outskirts of Amsterdam. His wife, a friendly, open woman in her thirties with blond hair, greeted us warmly and seemed not at all nervous at having us in her house. I think she found it hard to believe that I was involved in such a venture. She seemed impressed by us both and took a personal interest in our welfare. We went through Dave's briefcase, my handbag, and all our pockets, searching for any kind of incriminating material. We tore up every scrap of paper with any kind of information on it and flushed it all down the lavatory. All this time Dave and I remained convinced that we would be picked up, especially when the late television news had a full item on the arms find at Schiphol, showing Inspector Winslow of Scotland Yard examining the spoils, all 166 crates of them, including bazookas, rocket-launchers, and hand grenades. Dave was very upset at seeing the arms in the hands of the enemy, and so was I.

Jan asked us what we planned to do. We said we had no real plans. He pointed out that on Sundays there was considerable traffic between Holland and Belgium, because in Belgium many of the main shops remained open. He had heard that there were checks on all the roads out of Amsterdam, but if we travelled with them, with his two children on our laps, we'd have every chance of getting away. We passed the night in great anxiety, feeling sure that the house would be raided, listening nervously for the noise of approaching vehicles, wondering what would happen to the Dutchman and his wife. There was a Volkswagen parked some way away within sight of our window, and Dave became convinced there were people in it watching us. We kept our clothes on all night. I slept for about an hour, and Dave didn't sleep at all.

We heard more news of the arms find in the morning. We heard that a girl was involved, but I wasn't mentioned by name, and even though there was a full description of the clothes I wore, Dave was hoping I still had a good chance of getting away, even if he didn't. We left at eight, and, although we saw some police cars, there were no roadblocks to negotiate. During the journey we picked up a news bulletin on BBC radio. It said that the Dutch police had issued four arrest warrants, one for Dave, one for me—still unnamed—one for Freeman, and a fourth one for another unnamed person. I was afraid it might be Tom. An American called Koenig had already been taken in custody off the plane, along with the pilot. We had no idea who Koenig was, and I still do not know. (He was released a week later.)

We crossed the border into Belgium without difficulty—the customs man waved us on, just as they do between the Six and the Twenty-six Counties—and Jan took us on to Antwerp and dropped us at a shopping centre crowded with people. We said good-bye to Jan and his wife and thanked them for all they had done. I was wearing a miniskirt, which, being very short, was cold and also seemed to attract attention. I changed into trousers and put on a pullover I bought in the market.

We had no idea then how we were going to get home, or how to contact Dublin securely. We learned later that the Army Council had been laying contingency plans to kidnap the Dutch Ambassador in Dublin in case we were arrested in Holland; a Provo dressed as a milkman had actually cased his home, and the plan had been well developed.

Meanwhile we intended to head for Brussels at once. From there we could go to either Paris or Ostend. All we had in mind then was to get as far away from Amsterdam as we could, to somewhere where we could take stock of our situation and make calm decisions about what to do. We caught a train from Antwerp to Brussels.

Brussels station was not crowded, and we soon noticed that we had picked up two Belgian plainclothes policemen. They watched us as we bought tickets to Ostend, and then went to the ticket window afterwards to ask, presumably, where we were going. We found two seats on the Ostend train—and then the two men following us got on and sat opposite us. We were beginning to wonder if we were mistaken about them, if we were just becoming paranoiac in imagining everybody was watching us or following us, when they began talking, in French about the Amsterdam case. Then one of them took out his police identification and flicked it open as if casually—but making quite sure that we saw it. We realized that they wanted us to know who they were and that they would be sticking with us throughout our journey. Both Dave and I thought separately that they didn't want to arrest us and that they were just seeing us out of the country. But we couldn't be sure. At Dave's suggestion we went along the train for coffee, leaving our cases in the luggage rack. The train stopped at a station; then, just as it started to leave, we left the buffet car by the far door and jumped off. We lurked behind a pillar until the train had disappeared.

I hadn't been as keen on going to Ostend as Dave, and now we decided to head southwest, to France. I went into the station office to ask if there were any trains for France that afternoon and was told one was just leaving; we hastily climbed on. We had no tickets, and when the ticket inspector came into our compartment there was a bizarre misunderstanding. Dave said that we wanted to go to the border—we had decided that, as we had no false papers, it would be safer to cross by taxi—but it seemed as though the ticket inspector thought we wanted to bribe him to take us over the border. Even though we were still carrying nearly £20,000 with us, we certainly didn't want to do anything as risky as that and managed to persuade him of our entirely legitimate intentions.

We got off the train when it stopped at the Belgian border town, had coffee, and then took a taxi into France. It was easy enough: I simply smiled at the French border official; he smiled back and waved us through. We went to the railway station and took the first train that left. It happened to be going to Rouen. It would have been nice to get to Paris that night, but I was just tired of waiting for trains by then. We spent the night in a hotel in Rouen, in a square near the railway station.

In the morning we decided to go to Le Havre. It so happened that Dave knew a man there, a former sailor who was working in the Le Havre harbour control. Dave had been on holiday to Le Havre the previous summer with his wife,

Deirdre, and had made friends with the man and his wife, who kept a small hotel. It seemed ideal for us, offering safe accommodation and the possibility of getting out of the country.

We bought French and English papers in Rouen that morning. Dave's photograph was in almost all of them, and I was named as Moira Maguire; this misspelling was because the Dutch police hadn't managed to read my signature in the register back in the Hotel Delphi in Amsterdam. We were pleased to learn, though, that we were thought to be still in Holland. But it was only then that we realized the extent of the publicity we had attracted. Dave thought it was funny: "The lads are going to be amused by this back home," he said.

The newspapers seemed less interested in why we had gone to Amsterdam to buy arms, and the cause they were for, than in the relationship between Dave and myself. For Dave and I had been having an affair from the time I arrived on the Continent. It just happened and seemed perfectly natural, even though our situation was very unnatural. We were under considerable stress together and became very close, depended on one another, because of that. Possibly it meant more to Dave than it did to me; but when we managed not to worry about the outcome of our mission and our own chances of escaping, we were very happy.

When we arrived in Le Havre we went to the hotel, where the French dock official and his wife remembered Dave from his holiday the year before. But they didn't connect him with the arms deal. Dave explained to them that we were wanted by the Dutch police and that there were probably Interpol warrants out for us as well. The Frenchman said there was no problem. We could stay at the hotel, and there were two or three Irish ships into Le Havre each week. He would ask the captain of the next one if he could take us home. That was on Monday; the next day he told us an Irish boat was due on Wednesday.

As we waited, the tension grew. On Wednesday morning we

heard that there was a storm in the Channel and the ship would be delayed by eight to ten hours. We sat in our hotel room, rain beating on the window, and kept going over and over what had happened. What had gone wrong? Who was at fault? Were we? And, assuming we got back to Ireland, what would be the reaction of the Army Council to our failure? How would Dave's position be affected? Dave was acting more and more peculiarly, chain-smoking, pacing up and down, lapsing into long silences, staring out of the bedroom window at the rain. I was wondering whether to say, "What the hell's the matter with you?" when suddenly he blurted out, "Are you a British agent?"

I was stunned. "What do you think?"

"Well, it's possible. . . ."

Then it all came out. It was something people had suggested jokingly before—especially because of my sudden arrival from Spain, and the way I had come to know the Provisional leaders so quickly.

The question had obviously quite seriously been preying on his mind. Why had I laughed at the report in the *Daily Telegraph* that signalled the end of our mission? But I was very upset that he should ask me. I just said, "No," and looked out of the window. Soon afterwards Dave said he was going out for two hours—he was specific about the time. He left me with the money, and it was very obvious to me that if I wanted to go I was free to do so. I'm sure that he was giving me this opportunity because of his personal attachment to me, when by the rules, if he really believed I could be a British agent, he should not have done so. But if I had gone, it would at least have confirmed his suspicions and given him a neat explanation of why things had gone so badly.

I didn't go. When Dave came back he was relieved to find I was still there—he was so relieved that he actually said so, and he apologized. He joked too, saying that he wasn't worried by the newspaper reports of how many beds had been used, so long as they didn't discover all the whisky bottles underneath them. (Mac Stiofain had once actually stipulated there was to be no drinking on duty.) Afterwards he was much calmer; the crisis between us seemed to pass.

We waited throughout the afternoon for the Irish cargo boat to come in. In the evening we heard it had put in, and Dave went with the Frenchman to see the captain. The captain said he could take us that night. The Frenchman said he could get us through the French customs without difficulty. At 6:30 he drove us on to the quayside, past the customs, to very close to where the boat was tied up. On the quayside was a line of large steel containers. There were customs officials still on the boat, and the Frenchman indicated to us that we should hide in one of the steel containers. It was black inside and very cold, and we sat and shivered. After half an hour we came out and found that the customs men had gone. Hoping no one would notice, we boarded the ship by its gangplank leading from the quay to a gap in the deck rail. I followed Dave down some stairs to the captain's cabin.

As soon as we were inside I realized something was wrong. All the previous Sunday's papers were spread over the captain's table, Amsterdam headlines prominent. He was a stout florid-faced man, and he wouldn't look us in the eye. All he said was "I can't take you." You could smell the fear.

I just turned on my heel and walked out. I had utter contempt for him. He was Irish and so obviously afraid—and so many foreigners had helped us at risk to themselves. Dave tried to argue with him, but it was no use. When the crew saw us leaving again, they were annoyed that the captain wouldn't take us, but he was adamant. Afterwards Dave said the Provos would have their revenge. "He'll be got," Dave muttered. He may just have been venting his own anger.

We were now in quite a predicament, stranded at the dock inside the customs barrier. A car passed, and I simply stopped it and asked the driver if he could take us back to the centre of

Le Havre. The man seemed surprised, but agreed. He asked if we had just come off the boat, and I said we had. When he asked more questions about the voyage, I pretended not to understand. We passed through the customs control, and he dropped us in the centre of the town. We made our way back to the hotel, where the Frenchman and his wife were surprised to see us. They were upset too that, after everybody's trouble, we were still no nearer home. They brought out some wine, and the Frenchman's wife cooked a fine meal.

In the morning we decided to head for Paris. We were being followed again, I was sure, and at one point thought seriously about using my gun on one of our shadows. Our nerves were very taut by now. But in Paris Dave remembered the name of the *Irish Times* correspondent there, Fergus Pyle. He obtained his address from the office of *Newsweek,* and we went to Pyle's flat and introduced ourselves. Pyle just said, "You've had a long trip—have a drink."

What interested Dave most was the reaction in Ireland to what we had done. If we managed to get on a plane to Dublin or Cork, what would happen when we arrived? Would Lynch take any action against us? Pyle showed us all the Irish papers, and they seemed to be telling the story without undue hysteria. Dave was pained by one report which recalled that while interned in the Curragh he had been known as "the Cardinal" because of the puritan image he affected, never swearing, apparently uninterested in women. He was also known as"Mise Eire" —Irish for "Mr. Ireland"—because of the obvious strength of his Republican feeling. Was this the man, the report asked, who had been spending money all over Europe in the company of a young woman? None the less Dave thought the risk of Lynch's arresting us was slight, and we decided to take the chance.

In the morning we went to Le Bourget and bought tickets for a flight to Cork. We went through passport control separately; I boarded the plane first and watched Dave follow me. He sat down beside me, and as we took off we knew that the worst that could happen now was that we would be stopped in Cork. But I knew that Dave was already worried about what the judgment of the Army Council would be on our failure and whether his own standing would be affected.

We landed at Cork; I went through the customs and passport check with great ease. I was carrying all the money and both our guns—we thought it more important that Dave be clear rather than me—but the official simply asked me whether I was a foreigner. I nodded, and he wished me a pleasant holiday. But as I went through I noticed that Dave had been stopped in another queue. An official was going through his passport page by page, making notes. And through the barrier I could see two Special Branch men in a state of obvious agitation. One went off to make a phone call and then returned, and they kept a steady eye on Dave.

We had arranged to meet at a house in Cork, so I took a taxi there. Ten minutes later Dave arrived. We thought the publicity we had attracted must have safeguarded us: Lynch would not have dared move against us in the face of it. All he could have done, in fact, was to agree to our extradition, which would have been disastrous for him. The IRA remained popular in the Twenty-six Counties, and the Amsterdam episode fitted in perfectly with the public's conception of the Republican movement. The press had made great play of the fact that we had escaped the British secret service; we had achieved another glorious failure. It was better even than if we had been successful, because then the public would have had to confront reality. Why did we want the guns? To kill people.

We were a great attraction at the house in Cork, and a dozen or more Republicans called to see us there. I felt as though I was on display. Someone hired a car for us—we thought it better to keep our cover—and we left for Dublin early that afternoon. Along the road we stopped at a café—Dave was very hungry, and I wanted coffee—and on the television were the proceedings of the Ard Feis, the annual conference of Sinn

Fein. Most of the leading Provisional figures would be there, including Sean Mac Stiofain. Then we learned that Dave had been elected vice-president of Sinn Fein. He seemed very popular at the conference, undoubtedly because of the publicity he had received through the Amsterdam affair. It did not seem to matter that we had failed.

Dave left me at my parents' house in Dublin. When I went in, my mother and father both started crying; I looked at them in amazement. A few minutes later Joe Cahill and Ruairi O Bradaigh arrived. They hadn't realized I would be there, and they were crying too. They had, I learned, been up to the house almost every day to reassure my parents that I would come to no harm. They didn't always succeed. Once my father lost his temper in front of them and said he would "kill that idiot from Cork"—meaning the warehouse man—"with his bare hands." Another time Joe said casually that we would have no problem getting home—we'd just fly from Prague to Havana and then to Shannon, as if that was the easiest thing in the world. My parents certainly weren't convinced. Joe and Ruairi asked me how I had got on, and I just said, rather unimaginatively, that it had been an interesting experience. They didn't realize, until I told them, that Dave had arrived home safely too, and they found it hard to believe.

The next day, Sunday, was the second day of the Ard Feis. I had arranged to meet Dave at the Russell Hotel at lunchtime, and from there we drove up to Jack McCabe's house in Ballymun—Joe Cahill lived there too. When we arrived, Mac Stiofain, Ruairi, and Joe were preoccupied with the question of whether Dave and I should make an appearance at the afternoon's proceedings of the Ard Feis at Dublin's Liberty Hall. Ruairi and Joe both wanted us to appear on the platform, assuming that it would be helpful publicity for the movement and would also encourage the Sinn Fein delegates. But Mac Stiofain was against it. He said he was afraid the Irish Special Branch might attempt to arrest us there, which would lead to a fight in the convention hall. This did not seem realistic to us: Lynch would hardly make such a provocative move in front of so many Republicans, especially as there was so much apparent sympathy for us. We were sure—and later Ruairi and Joe confirmed it—that Mac Stiofain was anxious that Dave in particular should attract no more publicity. He was already becoming dangerously popular in Mac Stiofain's eyes. That afternoon Mac Stiofain made a highly charged speech, declaring, "Our fight has moved from a defensive to an offensive campaign in all parts of the occupied areas of the North." Dave wasn't interested. He had been so angered by Mac Stiofain's refusal to let him appear that he had just walked out of Jack McCabe's house. He was depressed too that the power struggle had been so promptly and obviously renewed. Mac Stiofain told us to keep out of sight, but Dave said to hell with it. We had always promised ourselves that if we ever got back to Dublin from the Continent we would go and drink whisky in the Shelbourne, Dublin's best hotel, and we did.

But we had by no means yet finished with Amsterdam. On Sunday, an article had appeared about me in the London *Observer,* after the Provisionals had denied consistently, while we were on the Continent, that they knew anything about me. It had been written by Colin Smith, the reporter who had visited me in hospital in August and who had done some astute detective work in Dublin and in Holland. The *Observer* published a photograph of me, which Smith had taken, too. On Monday and Tuesday press and television reporters besieged my parents' house, and it was impossible for me to go out. Dave had not yet been home to Donegal to see his wife, Deirdre, and he suggested I go with him. Given our affair, I thought this a strange suggestion, but I was so anxious to escape from the press that I agreed. Dave, in fact, went a few days ahead of me, and a friend of Dave's drove me there. Ruairi—he and Deirdre were first cousins—was staying with us too.

On the Continent, Dave had said he was going to tell Deirdre about our affair. At the time I dismissed this from my mind—I just didn't take him seriously. But when I arrived at his house I had no way of telling what his wife might know. She greeted me warmly and kissed me. That night we talked together pleasantly enough, although there was some tension between Dave and Ruairi. Ruairi said that if I ever told the press about my part in the Amsterdam operation I'd end down a bog-hole. I wasn't worried, I said—to which Ruairi replied that they could get at me through my family. I was sure that all this was said only half in jest, and Dave was angry at Ruairi for talking this way. But still nothing was said about our affair. But one night later that week we had been drinking, and quite suddenly Deirdre said, "Yes, Dave has told me all about it." She and Dave started to discuss the affair. I did not want to participate and listened as if a member of an audience—even though I had a central part in the drama under discussion. Dave had even suggested that we should have a baby together, which Deirdre would bring up—and in this, said Deirdre, Dave was not being fair to me. Although we were making a pretence of talking about the affair as sensible, rational adults, we were all very tense. Then Deirdre passed out and Dave put her to bed. He and I stayed up until the morning, talking things over.

It was not possible to dismiss the affair as something private, for it had a direct bearing on the leadership struggle within the Army Council. There was a real danger that if it became public Mac Stiofain would use the affair to discredit Dave. "Don't give the bastard any chance to get at Dave," said Ruairi.

Dave was saying stubbornly that he didn't mind who knew about it, that if any newspaper reporter asked him about it he'd tell him the truth, but Joe Cahill, Ruairi, and I were certain that Dave could be seriously damaged by it. Ruairi and I returned to Dublin to give a press conference—or rather a press statement, for I had no intention of being questioned in detail about either Amsterdam or my relationship with Dave.

So I went before the press at the Moira Hotel in Dublin and

simply read a statement which said two things: first, that we had been on the Continent to help import arms from Czechoslovakia into the Six Counties; second, that my relationship with Dave O'Connell was one purely of business. I said I would answer no questions; and Ruairi said that if the British press continued to pursue me, my parents, Dave, or Dave's family, "action would be taken against them." He did not elaborate on this threat; it was one that the Provisionals customarily made.

Only once did I hear of such a threat actually being carried out. The action was taken by Mac Stiofain himself, after an Irish journalist had written an article which would have enabled people to identify Mac Stiofain's house in Navan. Mac Stiofain called at the journalist's house and, when the man answered the doorbell, dragged him out into the street and gave him a good punching. (Mac Stiofain confirmed this incident himself, which I had known about while I was still in Dublin, in an interview published in the *Observer* after I had left Ireland for England in August 1972.) Other journalists naturally learned of Mac Stiofain's attack, and it had an effect on at least one, for when the Provisonals accused him of breaking a confidence (I don't believe that he did, and that there was a simple misunderstanding) he immediately went on holiday for four weeks, then changed both his flat and telephone number in Dublin.

Sadly, although Ruairi was with me on the occasion of my press statement at the Moira Hotel, there was no doubt that his relationship with Dave had been affected by the affair and by the anguished discussions that followed it. For some time afterwards Deirdre often became hysterical, and she cried a lot too. Ruairi was never as close to Dave as he had been before we went to Amsterdam, and this was another factor which was to help Mac Stiofain in his campaign to dominate the Army Council.

A week after the press conference, the Army Council conducted its own court of inquiry to examine the Amsterdam affair. Such inquiries were always held by the IRA to look into possible cases of ineptitude or betrayal. The court could recommend a member for court martial; and if then found guilty of treason he—or she—would be shot.

I had no such worry before the court of inquiry, even though Freeman, the arms-deal contact, had returned to Dublin and told Dave, Joe, and Ruairi that he thought I was a British agent. The three had talked the matter out and decided that I wasn't—and in fact they suspected Freeman himself for a time. Why had he asked for a fee of only £500 for setting up the arms deal with Omnipol? The night before the court, Dave, Ruairi, and I spoke at a party policy meeting at Donegal; by now Dave and I were star attractions in the Provisional movement. The court was held at a small semi-detached house in Dublin, and all the witnesses had to wait in a small front sitting-room for their turns to appear. There were nine or ten people in there, including Mac Stiofain, Ruairi, Joe Cahill, and John Kelly, as well as Dave and myself. We were not supposed to discuss the case with each other, or talk about any of the people involved. There was little else on anyone's mind, so the room was largely silent. Some people stared out of the window, while others went to sleep. Mac Stiofain made pot after pot of tea—another rule of the inquiry was that we were not allowed to drink alcohol.

When I was called, I went into the adjoining room and took an oath of truthfulness on the Bible. The three judges, nominated by the Army Council, sat behind a dining-table. One was middle-aged, two were in their thirties, and all three wore typical IRA suits, styled in the 1950s. They were friendly and smiled at me. Afterwards they told Ruairi what nice witnesses they'd seen—"It's changed times," one said. Their line of questioning seemed strange, mostly directed at what I thought of how other people had behaved. How had Tom, the Donegal shipping man, reacted, for example? Did he seem afraid? Did I think he could have talked? Did I think Freeman could have talked? They asked me if I had felt afraid at any point. I thought it strange that they should be seeking more for my opinions than to establish what had actually happened. The only question about my own movements was in connection with my return to Dublin from Zurich: had I talked to anyone about what was happening? Then the judges said they had finished, and I went out.

Dave was waiting for me in the hall. He thought I would be upset (I wasn't) and told me to go into the kitchen. He offered me a cocktail made of whisky and potheen. Sean Mac Stiofain came into the kitchen with a cup of tea in his hand. We offered him some potheen, but he said he preferred his tea. Later Dave said he had had enough of the court of inquiry and suggested we leave. As we went out the door together I heard Mac Stiofain say, "If those two don't watch out they'll have to give another press conference." It was the only joke I ever heard him make.

The findings of the court were made known a month later. They were "inconclusive," Joe Cahill reported to us; the court simply didn't know what had happened. Dave and I had talked over a number of times what might have gone wrong. We were sure that the large number of people who had learned something of the deal had been a major factor in its breakdown. In December, for example, Ruairí and I were invited to a Republican dinner at Tralee in County Kerry—we were guests of honour. I was astonished to hear from several people there that they had known we were on a deal while we were still on the Continent before the news even broke, and that it was "something to do with bazookas." Somebody, somewhere, must have talked, either knowingly or unknowingly, to a British secret-service contact. But how to explain the mysterious paragraph in the *Daily Telegraph?* We thought it must have been planted there by the secret service to move either Scotland Yard or the Dutch police to action, when either for reasons of their own had been hoping the deal would not come to light in a blaze of publicity. We had no inside information to enable us to make any firm judgment, and in this complete air of uncertainty rumours began to flourish, directed particularly against Joe Cahill and Dave. One we heard being circulated was that Joe, Dave, and I had sold out the deal in an attempt to keep the money for ourselves. The one man helped by the rumours was Sean Mac Stiofain.

The final episode in the affair was bathos itself. In November I happened to hear a television news item that two Irish citizens had been excluded from Switzerland—Dave O'Connell and myself. We had done nothing illegal in Switzerland that I could recall—although I remembered only too clearly our performance changing our Irish notes into Swiss money. Then the Swiss Embassy in Dublin telephoned Dave and asked us to call at the embassy to collect our exclusion orders. We naturally refused, and mine arrived by registered post. It was a pink pro forma, printed in French and German. Taking no chances, the Swiss had referred to me by four different Christian names— Maria, Moira, Maire, and Marion. The reason for our exclusion, quite blandly stated, was "traffic in arms"—and an interesting change had been made to the form's small print. The penalty for being found in Switzerland was normally twenty-eight days in prison, it seemed—but this had been crossed out in ink and replaced by "three years." Dave and I called at the Swiss Embassy to protest. The ambassador was quite sympathetic but said there was nothing he could do. He did offer, however, to supply us with literature about Switzerland's own form of regional government, if we were interested.

# 6

# An Offensive Campaign

*. . . there was always admiration
for fine examples of marksmanship.*

When I returned from Amsterdam I began to help Ruairi O Bradaigh more and more, looking after our contacts with the world's press and assisting him and Dave with the drafting of our statements. Ruairi was now emerging as a personality in the press and on radio and television, a development resulting directly from a fit of pique by Jack Lynch. On September 27, Lynch had met Heath and Faulkner at Chequers, in a further round of the totally ineffectual talks that had begun at the beginning of the month, and a television report on the meeting on RTE had been followed directly by interviews with Sean Mac Stiofain and Cathal Goulding, leader of the Official IRA in Dublin. To Lynch, this appeared to give two rebels equal status with himself. Early in October he rather pointedly reminded RTE that under Ireland's Broadcasting Act it could not put out "material calculated to promote organizations using violence to achieve political ends." Even though it could have argued back, particularly on how the word "calculated" was to be interpreted, RTE knuckled under. But with the assistance of Ruairi

O Bradaigh it did find an alternative way of presenting Provisional policy.

It was not known at that time that Ruairi was a member of the Army Council; the only names known by the public then were those of Dave O'Connell and Sean Mac Stiofain. Ruairi's only public position was as president of Sinn Fein, Kevin Street, the legal, political arm of the Provisional IRA. So from then on it fell to Ruairi to appear on Irish television and radio to answer for the activities of the Provisional IRA. He always started by saying, "Of course, I am only speaking for Sinn Fein, but I do understand that. . . ." It was a polite fiction which everyone ignored. But it was because of the extra burden of work this gave Ruairi that he came to use me more and more. When Dave was chosen as a vice-president of Sinn Fein, he was hopeful he too would be able to speak for the Provisional movement in this capacity; but an RTE man he suggested this to told Dave that because of his notoriety over Amsterdam and because he was known to be a member of the Army Council "he had more chance of appearing on television to talk about modern art than about the policies of the Provisional IRA."

It was because of Lynch's pressure on the media that the movement's political campaign became increasingly important. The newspapers seemed to have been given "guidance" from the government too: they were now devoting more space to the physical effects of the military campaign in the Six Counties, and less to our political statements and goals. So we organized public meetings throughout the Twenty-six Counties to explain our objectives, the reasoning that lay behind the Five Points first put forward on September 5, and the ideas for a system of regional government that had been aired at the convention at Monaghan on August 21. I spoke with Dave at many of these meetings, held in the main squares or market places of Ireland's country towns or in the lounges or commercial rooms of their main hotels.

The meetings, Dave also thought, would help give the movement the political base he considered vital. He was anxious that the movement define its objectives in concrete terms, which was why he wanted to put across the proposals for regional government which the movement had formally adopted as its political goal. The Officials once accused us of being solely a military alliance, and to an extent they were right. The leaders would say that they wanted Ireland to be "free"—but what they all meant by "freedom" was likely to be quite different.

Sean Mac Stiofain had a vision of a united Gaelic-speaking Ireland; having taken the trouble to learn Gaelic himself, he no doubt thought that everyone else could and should. But he did try to live by his own ideals; he had taught his own three children—all girls—Irish, much to the bewilderment of some volunteers from the Six Counties who had come south for a rest and stayed at Mac Stiofain's house. They couldn't understand a word, they told me afterwards. His interest in the Irish language seemed strangely obsessional. There was an occasion when a friend of mine was at a private house, helping to interpret for Mac Stiofain while he conversed with two groups, one French and one Spanish, from the Basque resistance movement ETA. They had come to offer us revolvers in return for training in the use of explosives, and my friend was struggling with words like "gelignite" and "detonator," when suddenly Mac Stiofain interrupted to ask her, "Have you Irish?" "Si," she said. "Er . . . yes." It seemed utterly perverse that in the middle of these negotiations this should be his only concern.

Mac Stiofain had a typically narrow Irish Catholic mentality that seemed at odds with the "new Ireland" the movement aimed to create. I remember his opinion of Conor Cruise O'Brien, the Labour member of the Dail who had been involved with Dag Hammarskjöld's United Nations operations in the Congo in 1960 and 1961. O'Brien had attacked us repeatedly in speeches in the Dail, demanding that Lynch move against us, close down the office, and arrest the Provisional leaders, and he once even took part in a demonstration against us in Kevin Street. Mac Stiofain seemed quite unperturbed at the danger O'Brien's attacks represented, and his only judgment on O'Brien, whose marriage had run into difficulty, was: "What kind of man is it who'll leave his wife and children like that?"

There was also an incident when the Provisionals' explosives experts were experimenting with contraceptive condoms to make acid fuses for bombs. The condoms were, of course, obtainable only in the Protestant North—but Mac Stiofain would never agree to bring a consignment back down with him after a trip. He would rather, it seemed, be caught with a Thompson in his car trunk than with a packet of contraceptives in his pocket — and it may well be that the movement would have been more horrified if he had been caught with a carton of French letters, too.

Ruairi and Dave realized the strength of Catholic feeling in the movement: they asked me not to tell anyone that I wasn't a Catholic myself, as it would again have upset too many traditional Republican supporters. I thought it supremely unimportant whether I was a Catholic or not. But I did realize the importance of their religion to the beleaguered inhabitants of the Catholic ghettos in Belfast and Derry; it may have been all they had to cling to. Dave said he was a Catholic himself, but I don't think he practised—at least when I knew him he didn't. Ruairi O Bradaigh believed he had direct contact with God, and this was a position many Provisionals had to adopt because of their constant feuding with the Catholic Church. On a number of occasions Cardinal Conway, Catholic Primate of All Ireland, condemned "terrorism", but when Ruairi and Sean Mac Stiofain asked to see him, he refused. Eventually Ruairi replied to Conway, asking why he had not also condemned the conditions in which Catholics were being held in Long Kesh. It was a bold move for Ruairi to make, given the movement's traditional Catholicism, but many members welcomed it, saying that a reply to Conway had been overdue. Mac Stiofain himself was probably the staunchest Catholic in the Provisional leadership —but then converts from Protestantism are always amongst the strongest Catholic believers.

Many members of the movement seemed to go in dread of Mac Stiofain; and to be chief of staff of the Provisional IRA was of course to be able to take life-and-death decisions. I remember one member of the Army Council had a brief affair with a close friend of mine; he was absolutely terrified that Mac Stiofain would find out. Mac Stiofain put it about, too, that he was teetotal—although he did in fact drink wine with his meals —and he also declared that the members of the movement should abstain while on duty. I was in a hotel in Dundalk where a Provisional meeting was being held, and I ordered myself a drink at the bar. Two Republicans were watching, and in a state of obvious anxiety one leaned over to me and said, "Mac's upstairs." He was clearly horrified when I said I didn't give a damn.

Dave O'Connell drank a lot, especially when he was worried —his favourite drink was Irish whisky, though he also liked white wine. (None of the Provisional leaders I knew drank Guinness.) Even so, Dave tried to stay in good physical condition. In the Curragh internment camp he had persuaded Ruairi that they should stay fit, which they did by running around the camp perimeter. But whereas Dave was still slim, Ruairi had developed a potbelly—as had Mac Stiofain.

It was fitting that Dave and Ruairi should have been so close by virtue of their shared experiences and dangers; I believed strongly that their strength lay in the coalition between them. Dave could grasp new ideas faster than anyone else in the Provisional leadership, but there was an erratic streak in his judgments, and he needed others to point out to him when he was no longer being realistic. Mac Stiofain disliked intensely being presented with ideas he could not understand; but Ruairi had greater patience and helped translate Dave's ideas into action.

Ruairi had a steadfast quality and a determination which

grew out of his own Republican background. His father had been badly wounded in a clash with the notorious Black and Tans, the British counter-revolutionary auxiliaries who had fought the IRA between 1919 and 1921; his wounds had needed constant attention, they had gone gangrenous, and he eventually died of them. Ruairi's mother took a second husband, a schoolteacher whom Ruairi disliked and so was not displeased at being sent away to boarding school. But there he rebelled against the rules that controlled every aspect of the boys' lives. He once described to me how the boys would take exercise by walking in a circle with their hands behind their backs. But Ruairi insisted on putting his hands in his pockets. Every time he came round, the priest in charge hit him, but Ruairi refused to take his hands out. His experiences there helped give him a passion—which he often articulated—for "justice."

It was essential, I saw, that he and Dave should stay together, particularly as the differences of opinion between themselves and Sean Mac Stiofain seemed to be growing clearer. Both they and Mac Stiofain knew that the movement's main dynamic was the military campaign in the Six Counties: it was the struggle there which gave the movement its strength. But how should the movement develop? Dave saw that ultimately the struggle would have to be translated into political terms, and that how successfully they managed to do this depended on the size of the movement they built up and the basis for unity it had. But Mac Stiofain seemed to believe that victory could be won by military operations alone. He was most at ease discussing military tactics, and had gone to considerable trouble to cultivate his power base among the fighting men of Belfast. His principal ally there was Seamus Twomey, a narrow, unimaginative man who had been interned at the age of twenty and until 1969 had managed a betting shop. Twomey had been with Mac Stiofain at the birth of the Provisional movement and had taken over command of the Belfast Provisionals after Joe Cahill had fled south following his defiant press conference in Ballymurphy. Cahill remained on the Army Council and was opposed to Mac Stiofain, but later his strength was to wane. In the months ahead the issues dividing the two factions on the Council were to be thrown into sharper relief, and the struggle between its personalities was to become increasingly open and bitter.

In the last four months of 1971, however, there was complete agreement about the military policy the movement should adopt (disagreement on actual military strategy, as opposed to the emphasis it should receive, was only to come well into 1972). When Mac Stiofain declared at the Ard Feis of Sinn Fein, held the weekend we returned from the Continent, that the fight had changed "from a defensive to an offensive campaign," his statement met universal approval.

The first British soldier to die in the Six Counties in the present campaign was shot by the Belfast Provisionals in February 1971. The main examples followed by the Provisionals in deciding to hit British soldiers were the guerrilla campaigns against the British in Cyprus in the 1950s and Aden in the 1960s. Algeria—although journalists often asked us this—was not a direct model, because of the indiscriminate civilian casualties the FLN caused. One book the Provisionals studied closely, with comparisons and summaries of these guerrilla campaigns and those of China, Cuba, Vietnam, and Israel among others, was *The War of the Flea,* a study of guerrilla warfare theory and practice, by an American writer, Robert Tauber. Ruairi O Bradaigh bought seven copies of the paperback edition and gave one to each of the members of the Army Council.

The Army Council's first target was to kill thirty-six British soldiers—the same number who died in Aden. The target was reached in early November 1971. But this, the Army Council felt, was not enough: I remember Dave, among others, saying, "We've got to get eighty." Once eighty had been killed, Dave felt, the pressure on the British to negotiate would be immense.

I remember the feeling of satisfaction we had at hearing another one had died. As it happened, the total killed by the time of the truce in June 1972 was 102.

The British soldiers were very vulnerable, as are any uniformed force in a guerrilla war. Our volunteers could recognize them; whereas they could never be sure who among the civilians around them was friend, who enemy. They naturally regarded themselves on hostile territory in the Catholic housing estates of Andersonstown, Ballymurphy, and the Ardoyne in Belfast, and moved there in strict patrol formation; even in the centre of Belfast they covered each other whenever they crossed a street, which they did at a run. But in areas like Andersonstown they were very clear targets: a sniper could fire a single shot with a modern weapon such as an SLR or an M1 carbine from a bedroom window a hundred yards away or more and then take cover and withdraw; or even stand up above a garden wall and pick off the last man in a patrol. A volunteer once told me it was like aiming at the moving ducks in a fairground shooting-gallery. Then there were the set-pieces: the hijacked buses that had been set on fire and would need clearing from across a street, when the troops covering the heavy army bulldozers could be fired on from half a dozen directions. Hitting the British Army helped morale in the movement both in the Six and Twenty-six Counties, and there was always admiration for fine examples of marksmanship—killing a British soldier with a single shot, or hitting one through the observation slit of a Saracen.

And having decided to intensify the campaign against the British Army in the autumn following Mac Stiofain's declaration, we were astonished to be presented with an ideal opportunity to hit at it in an entirely new area of operations.

# 7

# The New Year
# Border War

*. . . the day's one casualty*
*was a farmer's prize pig.*

As part of the political horse-trading that had gone on at their
Chequers meetings in late September, Heath had agreed to a
plan put forward by Faulkner for trying to prevent the IRA
from taking arms and men across the border. The border between the Six and Twenty-six Counties is 290 miles long, and
there are some twenty "approved" roads, with customs posts
across them, for crossing it. But there are also nearly two
hundred other roads where it can be crossed, with no customs
posts at all, and the only thing preventing people from using
them is a sign which reads "Unapproved road." In the most
peaceful times this was hardly a powerful sanction, and it was
certainly not one that was ever likely to have any moral sway
over the IRA. And so, proposed Faulkner, the unapproved
roads should be made impassable to traffic; this task would be
performed by the British Army, which would blow holes in
them with explosives. The plan was revealed to the world on
October 11.

It was an exceptionally stupid plan. It certainly would not

prevent our men from crossing the border; the British did not have the manpower to cover all 290 miles of it. It was bound to enrage the local population on each side of the border who used the roads, especially farmers, and involve a new group of people in the conflict. It would place the British Army in an extremely vulnerable position, carrying out operations in the same place for several hours, in country that suited guerrilla units ideally—with ample cover for firing positions, the opportunity to mine British patrol vehicles, and easily accessible sanctuary in the Twenty-six Counties. And the British were even running the diplomatic risk of a confrontation with the Irish Army.

The British Army started its cratering operations on October 12; on October 13 a soldier was shot and seriously injured at Roslea in County Fermanagh. On October 14 there was a two-hour gun battle between a Provisional unit and the British Army in County Armagh. All this, of course, had taken place during the later stages of the Amsterdam affair.

The men serving in our border units were mostly Republicans from the Twenty-six Counties. But later that year the units were strengthened by volunteers from the Six Counties—another ironic consequence of internment. The numbers of those held by the British had been rising steadily since August (the total was to reach 900 by March 1972). Men were either "detained" under Section 11 of the Northern Ireland Special Powers Act or "interned" under Section 12. The procedure was this. A man could be held for forty-eight hours before an order had to be signed detaining him; he then became a "detainee." After a further period of time—it could be four weeks, or even more—he would be either released or charged with a criminal offence, or another order would be signed and he would become an "internee." Eighty per cent of those held by the British at any one time were internees, the remainder detainees. It was one of those verbal niceties the British take such pleasure in, although it made no difference to the men themselves whether they were "internees" or "detainees"—they were still imprisoned without trial.

The Army had converted one of its bases into an internment camp at Long Kesh, just outside Belfast; a gloomy collection of huts behind a corrugated-iron and barbed-wire perimeter, with POW-style watchtowers at the corners. That was the main internment camp (a second was opened for a time at Magilligan, on the shore of Lough Foyle). There were 150 men held on a prison ship, the *Maidstone,* in Belfast harbour. And some men were held in Belfast's main civil prison in Crumlin Road, where the accommodation was under severe strain. In November, including convicted civilian prisoners, there were 900 inmates in Crumlin Road, twice the usual number, with only just over two hundred prison officers to handle them. When a gasoline-bomber escaped over the wall in the summer of 1971, it was the first escape from the prison for nearly ten years.

Then on November 16 nine men escaped from the prison. Two were recaptured quite quickly, but seven stayed free; they hid for a time in a Cistercian monastery in County Tyrone, we later heard. We heard of their escape on the radio and were naturally delighted. Then a day or so later, I was at a well-attended public meeting with Joe Cahill, Dave, and Ruairi in County Monaghan, when Joe was passed a piece of paper with the news that seven of the men had reached the Twenty-six Counties. When Joe, speaking last, announced this to the meeting, there were rapturous cheers. We appreciated then how much publicity and propaganda we could make from such escapes.

The seven men arrived in the Kevin Street office the following Monday—and, on seeing Dave, fell in before him in military style. A little embarrassed, Dave told them to relax. They told us of the treatment they had received in Holywood Barracks—known to Provos as the Holiday Camp—where the army conducted its interrogation of the men it held. They had, said one, been badly beaten and kept isolated; or, by contrast,

offered money or free holidays if they would give the Army information.

Reports of the brutal treatment the British Army gave to the
men it picked up had been coming out of Long Kesh within a
week of the Army's first swoop on August 9. Even though
Faulkner declared happily, "There has been no brutality of any
kind against either detainees or internees," the British government had set up a committee headed by Sir Edmund Compton
to look into these stories. In October the London *Sunday Times*
had published several articles on the British Army's interrogation techniques, based on statements smuggled out of Long
Kesh. The Compton Report was published on November 17
and it did its best to whitewash the British Army, as we had
expected. It went to great lengths explaining that what it had
found constituted "ill treatment" and not "brutality"—another
of those fatuous semantic quibbles which made no difference to
the actual experience of the men involved. But even so, the report did find that men had been deprived of food, water, and
sleep, had been hooded and subjected to continuous noise, and
had been forced to stand spread-eagled against a wall, in one
man's case for over forty hours in total.

In the wake of this report, we knew that a press conference
with the seven men who escaped would be powerful propaganda, and so we arranged it for Wednesday, November 25.
There was a party the previous night; one of the men drank so
much that he slept right through the morning and did not arrive
until the conference was over. Although the six who did turn
up were nervous at the television cameras, the conference was
effective and was well covered.

But the problem for us then was to decide what to do with
the seven men. For a time we let them rest and recuperate, and
we produced them at public meetings, where they were invaria-
bly loudly cheered as symbols of resistance to the British in the
Six Counties. But there was only one place they could be used on
active service: the border, where the Army Council had de-

cided it would step up its operations.

On December 2 came a further escape, and this time the British Army received a serious blow. The three who got over the wall of Crumlin Road were Martin Meehan, Dutch Doherty, and Hugh McCann. Meehan was commander of the Provisionals of the Ardoyne area, and he and Doherty were two of the toughest and most experienced volunteers in Belfast. They had been captured three weeks earlier, to the Army's delight, for the British had wanted to talk to Meehan about the shooting of three Scottish soldiers in Ligoniel in March. Under cover of the traditional football match used on such occasions, Meehan, Doherty, and McCann climbed over the wall on rope and knotted sheets. By the time their escape was discovered and roadblocks had been set up throughout the Six Counties, they had been in the South for hours. Newspapers speculated at the time that a prison officer must have connived at their escape, and this was undoubtedly true.

We held a press conference for Meehan, Doherty, and McCann in Dublin twelve days later, chaired by Sean Mac Stiofain, with John Kelly and Paddy Kennedy also taking part. We published a forty-page booklet called *Torture—the Record of British Brutality in Northern Ireland,* and Doherty and Meehan described their treatment. The day after the press conference the British Army said that Meehan had been a "mine of information" during questioning. It was a rather childish attempt to cause dissension among us, and we ignored it. We were more concerned about a remark made at the press conference by Paddy Kennedy, who said that Lynch couldn't take action against the IRA in the Twenty-six Counties because there was too much popular support for them. It was a pointlessly provocative claim, which we felt Lynch could not ignore, and it effectively ended the friendship that had existed until then between Kennedy and Mac Stiofain. On December 17 Lynch made a speech attacking the IRA.

There was a further press conference due on December 20;

this time it was the turn of the commander of the British troops in the Six Counties, Major-General Sir Harry Tuzo, to give his assessment of the campaign against us. And so, on December 19, we held our own press conference in Dublin, in which we said that our organization had not been seriously affected by internment, our supplies of arms and ammunition were still intact, and the British Army was powerless to prevent our operations. Naturally these claims were put to Tuzo the next day; our tactic of compelling other people to react to us, and not the other way round, was successful again. Tuzo said that the Provisionals had no coherent strategy and the Army was winning. His statements did not get the coverage he must have hoped for. We drove him off the front pages of the Belfast *Evening Telegraph* with a dozen bomb explosions in Belfast, demonstrating very clearly just who was winning in the Six Counties. There was a lot of pressure on us, some from the Catholic Church in the South, to declare a Christmas truce. The Army Council was against doing this publicly, feeling sure it would be seen as a sign of weakness. But the volunteers in the Six Counties were very tired by now, and word was discreetly passed that they could take a three-day rest.

Then both the movement and the group within it opposed to Sean Mac Stiofain received a severe accidental blow. One evening just after Christmas, Ruairi dropped me at home after a meeting, and I was getting ready for bed as I listened to the late news shortly before midnight. I heard that a man had been killed in a Dublin explosion; his name was given as Jack McCabe, the Provisionals' main explosives expert in the Twenty-six Counties and Joe Cahill's close friend. But the news item gave none of these details, as Jack was quite unknown outside the movement at that time. Then Dave phoned and said, "Jack's dead." The next day we learned how it had happened. He had been mixing chemicals in a lock-up garage that he rented close to his home. A shovel he was using scraped the concrete floor, a spark flew, and there was an explosion. It blew off the roof of the garage and Jack ran into the street, his clothes on fire and his face blackened. He called, "Get the children away" and then collapsed. He was taken, still conscious, to hospital, where he asked to see Joe Cahill and Dave O'Connell. Joe came; Jack's one concern was to tell him exactly what he had been doing and what he had done wrong, so that others would not make the same mistake. He died soon afterwards.

As the Provisionals' explosives expert, he had been experimenting with alternatives to gelignite, which the movement was finding more difficult to obtain as explosives stores in building and mining operations in the South were being more closely guarded. But—as the accident showed only too clearly—chemicals were more volatile. (Only a week before Christmas three Provos had died in an explosion in Magherafelt in County Derry, and a number of Belfast volunteers were to die using chemicals in 1972.) Joe Cahill was more affected than anyone by Jack's death, having stayed with Jack since his hasty retreat from Belfast after internment. After their part in organizing the abortive Amsterdam deal, the two had worked closely on the supply of arms and ammunition for the volunteers in the Six Counties.

The wake for Jack was held on New Year's Eve, Joe greeting people at the front door, Jack's wife and two daughters accepting condolences in the front room. The coffin was closed, because of the disfigurement Jack had suffered. I went with Ruairi O Bradaigh, and we placed our Mass cards on the coffin surrounded by wreaths and flowers, and knelt for a few minutes. Everybody in the Provisional leadership called at the house, and there were many down from Belfast too. We stayed at the house until three that morning, drinking tea. Many others stayed all night.

A day or so later we gathered again at Jack's house. There were too many people for us all to get inside, and the mourners spilled out into the front garden and the roadway, mingling

with the crowd of newsmen and television crews. Despite the
cold, there were many curious sightseers too. The honour guard
came out of the house, wearing black berets and green-and-
white armbands; the coffin was loaded into the hearse, and as it
drove off we followed it in ordered lines of three abreast. The
funeral was to be at Jack's birthplace, the village of Shercock
on the border between the Six and Twenty-six Counties in
County Cavan. We walked behind the hearse to the edge of
Dublin, then took a lift in a reporter's car back to the house,
where we had left Dave's Cortina. We caught up with the cor-
tège again, a long line of cars winding through the countryside.
It was a slow journey, with delays in every town we passed
through to take the salute from Provisional guards of honour.
At Shercock, the coffin was carried into the village church.

The funeral itself was to be held the following day; we drove
back to Dublin that night, and returned in the morning. After
the Mass we left the church to walk three miles to the graveyard. Special Branch was there, taking copious notes, as well as
the uniformed Gardai. The main question preoccupying the nu-
merous press and television men was whether there would be a
military salute over Jack's grave. We had been worried that a
salute would present Lynch with another opportunity to move
against us, as a volley of pistol fire could be interpreted as military action in the South. But Joe and Dave had argued strongly
that we should take the risk. Jack, said Joe, had served the
movement as well as anybody and had been in prison in England; there should definitely be a salute, he said, and so it was
agreed.

There were more than five thousand people walking along
the lane that led through the hills to the graveyard, and when
they crowded into the graveyard they filled it completely. The
Gardai and Special Branch were well to the back of the crowd.
Sean Mac Stiofain made an emotional and provocative funeral
oration, losing no opportunity to refer to the movement's present aims, and then without warning half a dozen men around

the grave pulled revolvers from their waistbands or inside pockets and fired into the air. The volley was a little ragged in its haste, but it was impressive none the less. At the back of the crowd the Gardai made a token move forward, but there were so many mourners that they were powerless to act: I don't believe they could even see who had fired the shots. Afterwards some T.D.s—members of the Dail—complained about the shooting, but Lynch took no action.

But Jack McCabe's death was to have repercussions on the manoeuvring inside the Provisional leadership. He had been a close ally of Joe Cahill in his opposition to Sean Mac Stiofain; and in losing a good friend and ally Joe was badly affected himself, too. For several months he lost a lot of his drive and was withdrawn and quiet at Army Council meetings. His passivity was another factor helping Mac Stiofain in his assumption of power.

In the New Year the border campaign, with the willing participation of Meehan, Doherty, and the other Belfast escapees, was pursued in earnest. There *had* been a confrontation between the British and Irish armies, and the British *had* lost several men killed by mines. The strength of local feeling over the British Army's cratering activities was shown by the serious rioting which had taken place just before Christmas at Ballyshannon, a town close to the border in County Donegal. Three Republicans from the Twenty-six Counties, including a popular local figure, Joseph O'Neil, had been arrested in the town of Bundoran after a border shooting incident with the British. Dave had been in Ballyshannon himself, and he told me it was quite clear that the townspeople had learned their rioting techniques from television reports on the battles in Derry and Belfast. He was anxious not to become involved himself and was very embarrassed when a truck loaded with bricks pulled up alongside him and the driver called out, "Here's some rocks—what do we do now?" Despite Dave's noncommittal answer, a great deal of damage was done to the town. (Afterwards Lynch limply blamed all the trouble on "outsiders.")

It had by now become a regular Sunday-afternoon pastime for local Republicans to fill in the craters made by the British, and the venues for coming weekends were even advertised in local newspapers. The carnival air was contributed to by the behaviour of the Northern volunteers, who lodged in Dundalk and always drank in the town's Imperial Hotel. The problem was that they had arrived in the Twenty-six Counties thinking they had come to paradise or Utopia, and they made little attempt to conceal the arms they always carried. Dundalk became known as El Paso. They played cards in the Imperial with their revolvers left casually on the card-table beside their stake money, were often drunk, and fought among themselves. The most notorious incident came when they were watching an afternoon race-meeting on the hotel's colour television set. One of the volunteers was so enraged when the horse he had backed lost that he shot up the television set. On another occasion, in Dublin, they were refused admittance to a discothèque; you can still see the bullet-holes where they vented their rage on the front door.

But their behaviour was a continual source of worry to us, for we were afraid it would finally provoke Lynch into action against the Dublin leadership. On January 15 Doherty was outraged at being arrested in Dundalk and charged with possessing a stolen car, and Faulkner immediately took advantage of the arrest by asking for Doherty's extradition to the North, where he was wanted for questioning about the shooting of two RUC detectives in Belfast in February.

Two days later came the most dramatic escape of all from the Six Counties, fully worthy of any British POW film. Seven men escaped from the prison ship *Maidstone,* moored in Belfast harbour, and they gave a full description of their escape at a press conference in Dundalk on January 23. They had covered themselves with boot-polish for camouflage, and butter for warmth, and then sawn a bar across a porthole which they had earlier filed halfway through. They slid down the anchor rope and then found a way through the barbed wire coiled around the ship; while watching from the deck, they had seen a seal come through it, and they made for the same place. They were all badly cut but felt nothing because of the cold. The 400-yard swim through the freezing harbour water took twenty minutes —they all stayed with the weakest swimmer of the seven—and when they clambered onto the quayside they hijacked a bus and drove into the Markets area of Belfast, a strongly Catholic district, where they promptly disappeared.

The men who escaped included several who became prominent in the campaign in Belfast in 1972. Two, named Bryson and Toland, were expert snipers from Ballymurphy whose photographs were pinned up in Army posts in the area. Tommy Gorman directed operations in the field in Andersonstown. All three were recaptured in Belfast in the autumn of 1972. The *Maidstone* escape, once again, was a superb propaganda coup for us, appealing directly to all that was most romantic and adventurous in the Irish Republican tradition. The same day as the escapees' press conference, there was another serious border clash; the British Army fired CS gas at sixty people who were filling in new craters.

On January 27 came the most prolonged incident of all, involving Meehan and seven other volunteers and a detachment of the Scots Dragoon Guards. There was a four-hour gun-battle over the border near Forkhill, County Armagh, the British acknowledging afterwards that they had fired 4500 rounds at the Provisionals' positions, although no one was hit on either side; the day's one casualty was a farmer's prize pig. Meehan strolled nonchalantly into Dundalk afterwards and, when a reporter asked him how he had got on, said happily, "We pasted them." The phrase appeared as headlines in the Dublin evening newspapers—giving Lynch another perfect excuse to move against the Provisionals. The next day seven men, including Meehan, were arrested in Dundalk and charged with possessing arms with intent to endanger life. It was a serious charge, and we wondered if it presaged moves against the Provisional leadership in Dublin.

But then came the incident which made any such move impossible for the time being, and which more than any other single event demonstrated the nature of the repressive policies of Stormont and the British government: Bloody Sunday.

# 8

# Bloody Sunday

*They walked into a massacre.* . . .

Even though the IRA had displaced it at the centre of the re-
bellion against Stormont, the Northern Ireland Civil Rights Association (NICRA) was still active in the Six Counties. Its demands remained reformist, as they had been in 1967 and 1968;
it protested at the denial of civil rights to Catholics, the
discrimination against Catholics in housing and jobs, the gerry-
mandering by which the Unionists maintained their dominance
in Stormont and especially in local government over the half-
million Catholics in the province. The NICRA would accept,
we always felt, a solution within the context of the Six Counties, whereas our object was to change the governments in both
Belfast and Dublin. For them, the border was not necessarily
an issue; for us, it necessarily was.

Thus when NICRA announced that it was to hold a march
in Derry on January 30 in protest against internment, we kept a
polite interest in how the NICRA leadership would react to
warnings from the Faulkner government that the march was illegal. For all parades in the Six Counties were prohibited, and
the government renewed its ban on January 18, only twelve
days before the Derry march was due to take place.

But the organizers went ahead, and both the Officials and

Provisionals in Derry agreed that for any demonstrators to carry arms would be a senseless provocation of the British Army. Ten thousand people joined the march, an impressive demonstration that they rejected the rule of the Unionists and the laws they would impose. They walked into a massacre. The Unionist government was equally determined to show that its supremacy was to be maintained. The First Battalion of the Parachute Regiment opened fire on the unarmed crowd, and thirteen men died, many of them shot as they ran for cover amongst the Rossville Flats of the Bogside, one of Derry's two main Catholic areas.

I was at home, that afternoon, watching television, when there was a sudden news flash saying that four people had been shot in Derry. With later news flashes, the total of dead continued to rise. It was very difficult to try to deduce what had happened, especially as there had been no intention by either the Officials or Provisionals to take on the British Army in Derry; an open confrontation may have been exactly what the British Army wanted, but we knew, following the classic theory of guerrilla operations, that it would be suicide.

Later that evening the BBC showed remarkable news films of the demonstration, showing paratroopers in action, demonstrators taking cover, the injured and dead carried away. In the morning the figures were confirmed: thirteen Catholics had been killed, fourteen wounded.

Reaction throughout the Twenty-six Counties was intense— and my own feelings were so strong that the next three days passed in something of a blur. Lynch's government announced that there would be a day of mourning on Wednesday, February 2, the day of the funerals for the Derry thirteen. On Monday, Bernadette Devlin, the young Westminster MP for the Six Counties constituency of Mid-Ulster, attacked British Home Secretary Reginald Maudling in the House of Commons after he had claimed that the paratroopers had "come under fire from a block of flats and other quarters"; and that the paratroopers had been "apprehending law-breakers with the minimum of force." If that was the minimum, we thought with a shudder, what could they do when they were really trying?

We received countless calls asking us what we were going to do—the first indications of the wave of support that Bloody Sunday was to bring us. Both the Officials and the Provisionals organized marches on the British Embassy in Dublin's Merrion Square, the focal point for three days of demonstrations that were to culminate in the embassy's being gutted by fire. Unions, schoolchildren, groups from most shades of the political spectrum, all came out on the street to protest, many of them carrying mock-coffins painted with the number 13.

Sean O Bradaigh called me on Monday to ask if I would speak at a public meeting we were to hold outside the post office on Tuesday night. I agreed, and on Tuesday, when the meeting was held, I had never seen O'Connell Street so jammed with people. After the meeting, which itself was cut short because it was so difficult to hold the crowd's attention, we marched to Merrion Square; the windows of British offices such as BEA were smashed, and the Dublin shopkeepers hurried out to put up their shutters. In Merrion Square, gasoline bombs were being thrown at the embassy, a tall house in an elegant Georgian terrace; I saw bottles curve through the air and smash against the wall, exploding in flames. Prominent in the crowd by virtue of their close-cropped hair was a group of Dublin skinheads who had found a load of coal to hurl at the embassy windows, but there were people of all ages, men and women, surging and cheering.

The real onslaught against the embassy came on Wednesday, the day of mourning throughout the Twenty-six Counties, observed with almost complete unanimity. There was another march on the embassy, with demonstrators carrying black flags and tricolours and three coffins draped in black, which were left on the steps leading into the embassy. There were probably twenty thousand people in the square, and the Provisionals' truck, from which some of the Provisional leaders including Joe Cahill were vainly attempting to make speeches and direct events, was quite swallowed up.

Then the gasoline bombs began again, raining against the embassy, each one greeted by a huge cheer from the crowd, which was behaving like spectators at a football match. The Irish police made an attempt to move it, a line of about a hundred charging with their batons drawn, and the crowd partly scattered. But it soon returned when the next gasoline bomb flew through the air. Some of the crowd were shouting, "Up the IRA"—how many would retain their enthusiasm for us in a week's time, I wondered?—and then chants began of, "Burn, burn, burn." Each explosion was greeted by a new cheer and a new surge forward. Then the window frames caught alight— but disappointingly, from the crowd's point of view, the flames did not spread inside the building.

Clanging bells signalled the arrival of the Dublin Fire Brigade, but its appliances couldn't get near the embassy because the crowd refused to move. When the firemen tried to approach down a street that led to the back of the building, they were blocked there too. The Gardai charged again, and made some impression on the crowd, but the next hail of gasoline bombs soon brought it back again, and from that time both the fire brigade and the Gardai abandoned their efforts. It was still pouring with rain—it had been for hours—and some of the more militant Provisionals now decided that, as there had been an attempt to burn down the embassy, they might as well see it through properly. I recognized among this group the Army Council member Paddy Ryan, a fiery, excitable man when aroused. It was he who had made the ringing declaration "We don't want lollipops, we want guns" that I had heard at one of my first Provisional meetings after internment. On Tuesday— the previous day—he had received a head wound from a Gardai baton charge in Merrion Square, which needed nine stitches. He seemed to have a knack of attracting trouble; on

TOP LEFT: *A civil rights demonstration in Derry became Bloody Sunday when British Army paratroopers shot thirteen men dead*

Photograph by Topix, courtesy of the London *Sunday Times*

BOTTOM LEFT: *On Bloody Sunday seventeen-year-old Hugh Gilmore (third from left) was shot in the stomach*

Photograph courtesy of Press Association Photos

TOP RIGHT: *The British Embassy in Dublin was fire-bombed on the third day that a crowd estimated at 25,000 had gathered outside to protest the Bloody Sunday massacre*

BOTTOM RIGHT: *The four-story embassy building was completely gutted because rioters lay in front of fire engines to delay their arrival at the scene*

Photographs courtesy of United Press International (UK)

another occasion he was driving out of Dublin when he saw a police car behind him. He thought it might be following him and so made an immediate U-turn, but completely misjudged the width of the road and, right under the eyes of the astonished patrolmen, drove into a field. Having now drawn far more attention to himself than if he had simply kept on driving, he abandoned the car where it stood, ran across the field, and disappeared on the far side.

For a short while, I lost sight of Paddy Ryan and the Provisionals around him, when suddenly I heard the news spread through the crowd: "The IRA's here." Then I saw a group of men moving quickly through the crowd, now wearing black IRA berets and carrying sledgehammers. I watched them attempt to batter down the door; to my surprise, they failed. (The door, I discovered later, was reinforced with steel.) Then several men climbed up the outside of the building, one with an axe, another with a tricolour. One tore down the Union Jack and flew the tricolour instead; there were more cheers, and a further barrage of gasoline bombs.

The embassy was still not burning, and it seemed as if our men were going to fail. Then, just as I heard someone shout the warning, "There's a bomb," there was an explosion at the front of the building and the front door fell in, injuring two members of the Special Branch who happened to be standing behind it. Gasoline bombs flew in through the doorway, and in minutes flames were leaping from the embassy windows. The crowd fell back because of the heat, ashes falling among it, but when the fire brigade moved in it found that its hoses had been cut.

All that week the burnt-out building was Dublin's principal tourist attraction. We thought it characteristic of British hypocrisy that the press and politicians expressed their horror and outrage at the burning—contrasting rather too acutely with their failure to express anything of the kind over the thirteen Derry killings. The Irish government, of course, apologized to the British—the British government hadn't apologized to Derry

—and said it would pay for the damage.

The British did announce an inquiry into the killings, to be conducted by Lord Widgery, the Lord Chief Justice, who would sit alone. It didn't seem important to us: we knew what had happened at Derry, and we assumed that Widgery would do his best to whitewash the actions of the Paras. We were more interested in the aftermath of Bloody Sunday, which brought us vastly increasing support and a large amount of money from inside and outside Ireland. We knew that we would be able to take increased action against the British Army in the Six Counties, and that it would be approved in the Twenty-six. Our only mistake was to announce that we would kill thirteen soldiers at once, one for each of the Derry dead. This we did not manage to do.

# 9

# Loyalist Backlash

*"We are determined to*
*preserve our British traditions. . . ."*

On February 3, Martin Meehan was remanded in court at Bal-
lybeg on the arms charges arising from the shoot-out a week
previously. But a new charge had been added: that of being a
member of an illegal organization. The charge was brought
under Ireland's Offences Against the State Act of 1939, drawn
up to deal with the IRA's bombing campaign of 1939 and
1940. Then, six days later, Meehan and the six others came before a court again, in Dundalk; and this time one man was released and the charge against Meehan under the Offenses
Against the State Act was dropped, on instructions from the
Irish Attorney-General. It was, we felt, a sign that Lynch was
no longer confident that he could move against the IRA, after
Bloody Sunday, and Wednesday in Merrion Square. A week
later all charges against Meehan and the others were dropped.

But then the pendulum swung the other way. On February
22 the Officials left a car-bomb alongside the officers' mess at
the English headquarters of the parachute brigade in Aldershot
(it was the Paras' First Brigade, which had shot the Derry thirteen). But when the bomb exploded it killed not Para officers
but five waitresses, one gardener, and an Army chaplain who

happened to be a Roman Catholic. That afternoon, before they even realized that they had killed the wrong people, the Officials claimed responsibility for the explosion from their office in Gardiner Place, Dublin.

I was in Kevin Street that day and helped prepare our own statement: we said we understood the reasons why the Officials had placed the bomb. But privately we felt that both the explosion and the immediate claim of responsibility from Dublin were appalling mistakes. In the first place, the Officials had bungled the operation: their intelligence had not even managed to establish just who would be in the officers' mess when the bomb was to explode. But more than that, it was our definite policy then not to take the war to England. We knew we would not be able to sustain operations there; on classic guerrilla theory you fight only where the population will support you and give you refuge. Previous attempts to carry the war to England had been equally disastrous and counterproductive. When the IRA killed five people and injured fifty-two with a bomb in the centre of Coventry in 1939 it lost immediate support in both Britain and Ireland, and two of its men were captured and executed. It was this campaign too which the Irish government countered with the Offences Against the State Act, used against Meehan only two weeks previously.

The Officials' second major blunder was to claim responsibility for the Aldershot explosion from Dublin. It was inevitable that the British government would put immediate pressure on Lynch to act against them; they should have made the claim from somewhere in Britain. The day after Aldershot there were widespread arrests in Britain, and at the same time—the swoops were obviously coordinated—Cathal Goulding, leader of the Official IRA, was arrested in Dublin, with seven other leading members of the movement. Another nine were arrested in Dublin the next day, and we seriously wondered if Lynch would move against us too.

The following day, February 25, the Officials tried to assassinate John Taylor, the Stormont Minister of State for Home Affairs. He was struck by at least four bullets, two hitting him in the neck, but had a miraculous escape. I remember the reaction in Dublin. I was in a pub with Dave when the news came through, and several people muttered such sentiments as "A pity the bastard didn't die." We were generally opposed to political assassinations too, much though we'd have liked to see Taylor, one of the Unionist hard-liners in Stormont, out of the way. In December the Officials had bungled yet another operation when they called at the home in Strabane of Senator John Barnhill, a right-wing Stormont Unionist MP, intending to wreck it as a reprisal, they said, for the terror used against the working class of the Six Counties. But Barnhill had put up a struggle and was shot; the Officials blew up the house with his body inside it. We felt that such activities only created political martyrs who would be used by the other side, and this was our judgment on the Taylor shooting.

And it was at this time that the Loyalists were grouping their forces in readiness for the changes that Bloody Sunday had made inevitable. Early in February the first talk had come of a British "initiative" in Northern Ireland, shorthand for the reduction of Stormont's powers that we were sure would come. The Loyalists perceived this too and prepared to defend the supremacist position they had held for fifty years.

On February 13 William Craig entered the scene again. As Stormont's Minister of Home Affairs in the late sixties, he had ordered the repressive measures against the Civil Rights Association that so played into the IRA's hands. In 1968 he had been sacked by the Stormont Unionist Prime Minister of the time, Captain Terence O'Neill, after making a pitch for the party leadership with militant statements about defending the Loyalist position. He now appeared as a focus for the increasing rumblings of Loyalist protest and on February 13 conducted a rally at Lisburn which, I thought as I watched a television report, had clear neo-Fascist resemblances. Craig walked among the lines of men in military order, pausing here and there to shake hands or pass a few words. He read a covenant pledging resistance to British reforms and then asked all those who agreed with it to raise their hands three times and call "I do." He also told the crowd, "We are determined to preserve our British traditions and way of life. And God help those who get in our way."

There was to be one recorded meeting between Craig and any of the Provisional leaders. It came when both Craig and Ruairi O Bradaigh flew to the United States for a televised debate on the future of Ireland. Others taking part included John Hume, the Social Democratic Labour Party Stormont MP for Foyle, the Catholic constituency of Derry; Basil MacIvor, a Unionist MP in Stormont; and Tom Connghty, Chairman of the Central Citizens Defence Committee, a group working for the welfare and protection of Belfast Catholics. After the debate, when drinks were flowing in the hospitality room, Hume played the diplomat and introduced Craig and Ruairi to each other; Craig offered his hand and Ruairi took it. But now the entire room fell silent, straining to hear what these two militants at opposite ends of the political spectrum could possibly have to say to each other. In such an atmosphere, Ruairi told me later, he could hardly open up a discussion of any political substance, and he asked Craig if he was now well, following a slight illness he had suffered. Then he asked after Craig's wife. Tentatively the conversation turned towards military matters, and Craig remarked that he had more rifles at his disposal than the IRA. At this point the Unionist MP Basil MacIvor offered the opinion that in the present situation no one individual was of any importance—not him, not Ruairi, not Craig. "In the face of such self-effacing modesty," declared Craig, "I'm going to the lavatory." As he passed Ruairi he muttered, "Leadership never abdicates its responsibility." With those words the historic encounter closed.

It did not come as a surprise to us, in February and March,

to see Craig emerge and the Loyalists organize so readily. It was natural that the Loyalist leaders would rally the Protestant working class to their defence, as they had done successfully ever since the country had been partitioned in 1920. What we did not know, as Craig stomped to rally after rally, was the strength of the Loyalist movement. The groups that became most prominent were the Loyalist Association of Workers (LAW) and the Ulster Defence Association (UDA), with Craig's Ulster Vanguard movement acting as an umbrella for the different factions. The most threatening seemed to be the UDA, whose members appeared on the streets in forage caps, with dark glasses and handkerchiefs covering their faces; we thought they just looked ridiculous, but at first wondered if they would be a serious military force. But then, as they seemed to spend all their time marching up and down, we became less concerned and judged that there was no real military depth behind the façade of parades and drill. Dave said that no Loyalists had ever fought out of British uniform—in contrast with the rebel traditions of the IRA—and that it would be psychologically very difficult for them to do so. In a way we were relieved at their appearance, because now we knew the strength of the opposition; Joe Cahill even said he hoped they would attack, because then we would be able to deal with them. It was only in May that these views were shown to be overcomplacent, when the UDA began seriously to affect the lives of Catholics in the Six Counties, and the talk shifted from "fear of the backlash" to "the danger of civil war."

Four weeks after Bloody Sunday a march was organized in Derry by two militant groups, the Northern Resistance Movement and the Derry Women's Action Committee. The march was to protest Bloody Sunday itself and to demonstrate continued and undeterred rejection of the rule of Stormont. The organizers asked if I would speak at the meeting at the end of the march, and I agreed. The march, like that of four weeks previously which had ended so bloodily, was illegal. But the government, which perhaps by now had learned the disastrous consequences of confronting unarmed marchers with armed paratroopers, let it be known that the march would not be interfered with. Even so, Dave O'Connell showed extreme anxiety for my safety and made all the arrangements for my visit to Derry himself.

I was on the "wanted list" maintained by the British Army —the roll of people they simply wanted to take in. (Apparently, simply to be on the wanted list was a crime in itself, such was the totalitarian nature of the British rule over the Six Counties. After Bloody Sunday the British Army had justified killing thirteen civilians by claiming that four of them had been on their list. Later, the Army admitted to the Widgery Tribunal that this was not true—not one of the thirteen listed.)

I travelled to Donegal with a Provisional from the Six Counties who was also going into Derry, and at a Provisional's house went through my bag to remove all evidence of who I was. I had with me a French journalist's press card to establish a false identity—because, although there was no pass system or wholesale issuing of identity cards in the Six Counties, British soldiers at roadblocks and at chance searches always asked for your "papers." It was far simpler to present a driving licence or similar document than to protest that you weren't obliged to carry "papers" at all.

From Donegal, we drove to Bridgend, a village just south of the border on the Derry road. From there we telephoned to a Republican's house in Derry. Following the safety precautions always taken, two volunteers drove down to meet us; we would follow a short distance behind so that if they came to a military patrol or a road block we would be able to halt or turn back inconspicuously. (I knew that there was a risk the British would recognize me, as my photograph had been pinned up in several Army posts, and at one was used as a dart board.) The volunteers reported that there were soldiers about; they disappeared and came back half an hour later to say that the road was now clear. From the border post—a customs man waved us through cheerily—to Derry was only a few minutes' drive.

Derry occupied a vital place in the mythology of the struggle in the Six Counties. Sixty per cent of its population was Catholic, yet from the way its ward boundaries had been drawn after partition its local council had always had a Protestant majority. The Catholics in Derry had always been seen as beleaguered inhabitants of a hostile land, the more so because they lived in two tight communities. One was called the Bogside, a mixture of narrow streets and modern flats immediately below the old walls of the city. The other was the Creggan, a drab, windswept housing development on top of a hill above the Bogside. In this unlikely location "Free Derry" had been created at the time of the RUC attacks in August 1969. Barricades of girders and wrecked cars were placed at the entrances to the two areas, barring admittance to the British Army and the RUC. The "No-Go" areas of Derry became a sanctuary within the Six Counties for the IRA, and a symbol of resistance to Stormont that by its mere presence encouraged Republicans—and infuriated Unionists and Loyalists.

We drove up the hill from the Bogside and passed through the barricade at the entrance to the Creggan, the girders impaled in the road like giant teeth. I was taken to a house in the Creggan where I met some of the other people who had come to Derry for the protest march and meeting—from the Civil Rights Association, the Northern Resistance Movement, and other non-IRA groups. After a time we went out to the Creggan's one pub, in the single square that forms the development's main shopping centre.

It was crowded there, and not very comfortable, and when we heard that there was a large group of people, including Bernadette Devlin and Frank McManus, in the Bogside Inn, the pub that was the Bogside's main gathering place, we decided to join them. It was now that I discovered just how anxious Dave had been about my visit to Derry, for when I said I naturally wanted to go down to the Bogside with everyone else, I was told I couldn't. Dave, I learned, had insisted that I was to stay out of sight, under cover, and run no risks at all—and he must have strengthened his request with severe threats of what would happen if anything went amiss. No, said the volunteers I was with, I definitely had to stay in the Creggan; and they took me to my lodgings in one of the grim council houses that made the Creggan the most depressing area I had ever visited.

Still miserable, I got up early in the morning to be ready for the march and meeting in good time. But the precautions taken to hide me away had apparently defeated the Provisionals themselves, for it took them several hours to track down where I was staying. It was pouring with rain, and the wind was sweeping through the Creggan. The march was strongly supported, with five thousand people following the route from the centre of Derry to Free Derry corner, at the entrance to the Bogside, where large black ornate letters spelled out: "You are now entering Free Derry." Frozen and soaked by the wind and rain, I was by now too numb to feel any emotion. A truck pulled into position, and I spoke first, referring to Bloody Sunday and declaring that we would go on to defeat the British Army. I was lifted down from the truck and was looking forward to going to the Bogside Inn with the other speakers—but there was a car waiting to hurry me back to the Creggan. I consoled myself with the thought that I would be back in Dublin that night—but then word came that there were roadblocks up and I would have to stay in the Creggan another night.

That evening a volunteer took me to meet a group of people in the Creggan who had wanted to tell Dublin what they thought of the way the campaign was being conducted. They were mostly middle-aged Republican sympathizers and they were very critical of the Provisionals' attacks on the men of the UDR, the citizens' militia which had replaced the notorious Protestant police auxiliaries, the B Specials, in 1969. One particular case in Derry ten days previously had disturbed them, when a local UDR member—a bus-driver—had been dragged screaming from his cab by hooded men and shot before the horrified young schoolchildren who were his passengers. We had met criticism of attacks on UDR men before, especially in rural areas where they would be well-known in the small local communities; and what made it worse to the people of Derry was the particularly public and brutal method of the killing. It had also caused the women of the Creggan much inconvenience, as the Derry bus-drivers now refused to take their buses into the development.

Some of the men too resented having to take orders from volunteers whom they remembered playing in the street as young children, and said they found them very arrogant. There was certainly a strong feeling of dissatisfaction with the Provisional campaign—but also one of hopelessness, for they realized that the Provisionals were still the best hope the Catholics of Derry had for improving their position. There was also, I heard, considerable feuding between families in Derry, with occasional shoot-outs, which was perhaps inevitable in their claustrophobic situation. I went back to the cold house I was staying at, feeling very low; Derry, romantic enclave of freedom within the Six Counties, was a totally miserable and depressing place.

I had to wait several hours to be taken back to the border in the morning, while the local Provisionals looked hard for a car that was "clean." The delay stemmed from the fact that all the Derry volunteers drove around in new, brightly coloured cars, mostly Cortinas or Avengers, that had been hijacked in the Six Counties. Many of these were known to the British Army and likely to be stopped on the road. But the problem of finding a car that was safe turned out to be beyond them, and in the end they took the risk of driving to the border in a hijacked car. I was met at the border, driven to Donegal, and caught the train to Dublin.

# 10

# Counterproductive Casualties

*The Abercorn restaurant was crowded*
*. . . when a small gelignite bomb exploded.*

I told Dave O'Connell of the dissatisfaction I had found amongst Republican sympathizers in Derry with some of the Provisionals' actions. He took my news seriously, for it had always been crucial to our operations that we should retain the support of the local Catholic population. We knew too that we had to compete for their sympathy with other groups—most notably the Social Democratic Labour Party (SDLP), whose continual manoeuvrings preoccupied the Provisional leadership more even than the military posturing of the Loyalist UDA.

We knew that our campaign against Stormont and the British was on the brink, in early March, of producing a major change from the British government (the long awaited "initiative" that had been talked of since early February). It was likely that the initiative would include some form of concession to the demands for civil rights with which the entire present campaign had started. At that point, would the SDLP present itself as the true representatives of the Nationalist population, accept the reforms on its behalf, and leave us with no political standing? We knew that the SDLP was not interested in structural changes in the Thirty-two Counties, only in limited reforms within the Six Counties. We knew too that the Catholics had been downtrodden for so long that they might well readily grasp at the thinnest of reforms. And we knew that, in that event, the SDLP would attempt to drive a wedge between us and the population that had supported us in our military and political campaign. If we were cut off from our support, Lynch would not hesitate to move against us in the Twenty-six Counties. These fears governed many of our actions both before and after the introduction of Direct Rule in the Six Counties.

It was most important of all, we felt, never to let it be thought that we were in a position of weakness—the reason why the Army Council had not formally called a Christmas truce, and the reason why our military activities had increased since Direct Rule; there were four bombs a day on average throughout the Six Counties, rising to peaks, as on February 11, when six exploded in Belfast. The killing of the UDR men was another concerted policy—the Derry man who had been dragged from a bus and shot on February 16 was the eighth to die; the ninth was killed on March 1. There was a clear risk, as I reported to Dave, that these killings were proving counterproductive; and on March 4 an event occurred in Belfast which also threatened our support. The Abercorn restaurant in the city centre was crowded with Saturday-afternoon shoppers, many of them women, when a small gelignite bomb exploded, killing two people and injuring more than a hundred, some of them losing limbs and being crippled for the rest of their lives. We did not cause this explosion, and the following day Mac Stiofain said that it had been the work of Protestant extremists. There was also the possibility that the explosion was the work of a freelance, although I did not consider this at the time; but whoever caused it, many people simply assumed it was the work of the Provisionals, and the casualties redounded to our discredit.

The Army Council did call a cease-fire on March 10 (the day when by coincidence the Official leader Cathal Goulding was released from custody in Dublin, sixteen days after being arrested in the aftermath of Aldershot). But the truce was not in response to any anger over the Abercorn explosion, and was in fact shortly preceded by a huge blast in Grosvenor Road in the centre of Belfast in which more than fifty people were injured; once again, the Provisionals were determined to demonstrate that they moved from a position of strength. The truce was a gesture to the increasing political contacts the Provisionals were having at that time. Despite our distrust of the SDLP, we had always kept in informal touch with it, reasoning that if the British government wanted to learn our views it would be to the SDLP that it would initially turn. (We were by now sure that the British government would be compelled to ask where we stood politically, such was the success of our military campaign.) More immediately, the truce was in tacit recognition of a forthcoming visit to Dublin by Harold Wilson. Dr. John O'Connell, a Labour member in the Dail, had asked us if we would meet Wilson, and of course we agreed. We were determined to lose no opportunity of putting our views across, and such meetings were always of considerable propaganda value, even though on this occasion Wilson asked that the meeting be kept secret. (News of it was later to be published, inadvertently, through Wilson himself.) Wilson was due in Dublin on March 13; we felt that it would demonstrate to him just how much control we had if we held the truce in the three days before his arrival, and we also recognized that it would make it easier for him to meet us if there was a lull in our military operations. There was an immediate pay-off, for in a television interview on RTE that night Wilson referred to us as a "well-disciplined, ordered, and tightly knit" force. I remember that the interview made a favourable impression in Dublin: people were impressed that he knew that the SDLP had left Stormont over the shootings of Cusack and Beattie. But we judged his performance more cynically: it was a typical piece of politician's opportunism, playing to his audience, and riddled with ambiguities.

Our judgment was confirmed when Wilson met Dave O'Connell, Joe Cahill, and John Kelly. (Neither Ruairi nor Sean Mac Stiofain was at the meeting because, it was put to us, for Wilson to meet the two acknowledged leaders of the movement would create diplomatic difficulties for him.) Dave told me afterwards that in political terms the meeting itself was quite unproductive. He had outlined the five points which had been proposed the previous September and explained the policy of regional government. Wilson seemed to be more concerned with creating a favourable image, behaving in a very hearty manner, slapping the three on the back and using such words as "bloody" and "Christ." Presumably he thought the Provisionals swore in this way. The Provisionals' public image, of course, was one of abstemiousness and moderation, whatever the private reality. "What kind of fools does he take us for?" asked Joe Cahill afterwards. The real coup for us came a week or so later when Wilson revealed that he had met the Provisionals. (To his credit, Wilson did send us a message first to say that the truth was going to get out.) It was a considerable propaganda victory for us that a leading politician like Wilson should have talked to us—however unproductive the talks themselves.

The truce ended on March 14. Mac Stiofain had made three basic demands: an amnesty for all Republican prisoners in Britain and Ireland; withdrawal of British troops from the streets and a date for their return to Britain; and the abolition of Stormont. Mac Stiofain said that, if these were met, the truce would be made permanent. They were not, of course, and Mac Stiofain announced that hostilities would be renewed; the one gesture from any direction had come from the British Army, which took advantage of the truce to arrest thirty-three of our men.

On March 20 came one of the worst explosions of the campaign, in Belfast's Donegall Street, when a car-bomb killed six men and injured 146 people. What was particularly unfortunate was that most of those killed had been cleared from another street by the Army and police and had thought they were safe. By now we were exploding four bombs a day throughout the Six Counties (compared with three a day in 1971), and incidents like this were the consequence of the increased security checks on pedestrians by the Army and RUC in Belfast. It was now very difficult to take a parcel-bomb into a shop, shout a warning, and then run, as anyone carrying a bag or parcel that looked at all suspicious was likely to be searched at any time. Dave had been one of the first advocates on the Army Council of the use of car-bombs, and these were now being used increasingly. Volunteers would hijack a car, place a bomb in the trunk or leave a parcel bomb on the back seat, drive it into the city centre, and leave it there. Another volunteer would then phone a warning. But it was this system that made civilian casualties more likely, for there were too many possibilities of misunderstanding as the warning was passed on.

On this occasion, however, the Provisionals directly blamed the security forces for the Donegall Street casualties, claiming that they had deliberately muddled the warnings in order to maximize casualties and discredit us. I believed at the time, and still do, that the Provisionals did not cause the casualties intentionally; but I now think it more likely that in Donegall Street they were a result of confusion or misunderstanding. Even so, despite blaming the security forces, the movement "accepted responsibility" for the explosion, and it was a curious thing that the Provisionals felt that by doing so they somehow atoned for the casualties, as if they had gone to Confession and asked forgiveness. I admit that at the time I did not connect with the people who were killed or injured in such explosions. I always judged such deaths in terms of the effect they would have on our support, and I felt that this in turn depended on how many people accepted our explanation.

On the day of the Donegall Street explosion, four bombs were sent through the post to the IRA—one to Cathal Goulding of the Officials, three to ourselves. Our treasurer, Tony Ruane, was badly burned on the face and hand when his went off in the Kevin Street office, and Mac Stiofain received a singed eyebrow when his exploded in his back garden at Navan. The parcel intended for Ruairi was intercepted by the post office at Roscommon. Goulding defused his with a metal coathanger. I had been with Ruairi that morning and left Roscommon by train for Dublin at midday. When he heard about the parcel-bomb, Ruairi telephoned my mother and said that if a brown parcel arrived by post, on no account to open it, but leave it in the middle of the garden. He offered no further explanation, fearing as usual that he might alarm my mother—but in fact leaving her in doubt and confusion that only served to disturb her even more. I did not receive a parcel.

For a long time afterwards Mac Stiofain wore a black eyepatch over his slight burn, which I thought made him look like a rather tawdry Moshe Dayan. (The Irish press summed up both the patch and his intransigence by christening him General Die-on.) This was unfortunate at a time when we were trying to persuade the world to take us seriously, I thought. (My opinion was eventually to be used against me by Mac Stiofain.) Mac Stiofain's wife, Maire, was genuinely very shocked by what happened—it was, she said, "a terrible thing for anyone to do." Her opinion seemed ironic—this almost harmless incident coming on the day six men were blown to pieces in Belfast.

Two days later, on March 22, came the long-awaited initiative: the British were to suspend ("prorogue" was the highflown word they used) Stormont for a year and rule the Six Counties direct from Westminster. William Whitelaw, until then leader of the House of Commons, was to govern the province. We had known that an announcement was coming that morning, and Ruairi and I went to the Kevin Street office to take it down and prepare a statement in response to it.

## Counterproductive Casualties

The moment itself was attended with bathos. Ruairi and I were listening closely to the radio, furiously scribbling down the wording of the announcement, when the telephone rang. It was a Sinn Fein official from somewhere in the country: what had happened to the Easter Lily badges he had ordered? Didn't we realize Easter was only ten days away? It was his one concern at the very point in time when the fifty-year rule of Unionist supremacy was coming to an end. Ruairi said—with great politeness, I thought—that he would try to find out what had happened.

Within half an hour of the announcement, a statement by Sean Mac Stiofain was being broadcast. It said that the Provisionals rejected the British government's move—none of the Provisionals' demands had been met, for Stormont had not been abolished, only suspended—and the Provisionals would continue the military campaign. As President of Sinn Fein, Ruairi knew that a statement would be expected from him too, so we drafted one together and phoned it across to RTE. It was broadcast at 1:30. At once Mac Stiofain rang in a rage. In the statement Ruairi, although very critical, had said that the suspension of Stormont was a "step in the right direction." How dare Ruairi take such a soft line? Mac Stiofain demanded; it was absolutely necessary for the movement to maintain a hard position.

Such castigation depressed Ruairi, the more so because Dave O'Connell and Joe Cahill, who had come into the office, agreed with Mac Stiofain. The bad feeling lasted all day. Of course, the proposals were totally for change within the Six Counties, but there was no denying that the end of Stormont— which is what the political commentators agreed had happened, whatever it was called—was one of our own demands. Ruairi had plenty of occasions to explain the subtleties of our position, as he was interviewed by many radio, television, and newspaper reporters and ended the day by appearing on RTE's *Seven Days* current-affairs programme. During the televised discussion much criticism was directed at Mac Stiofain, and Ruairi, in his usual ambiguous role, appearing as President of Sinn Fein but answering questions about the Provisionals, did his best to defend him. Eventually he said that he didn't think it was fair to attack Mac Stiofain in this way as everyone knew that Mac Stiofain was prohibited from appearing on the programme to answer back. Afterwards Joe Cahill telephoned Ruairi to congratulate him on his performance. "Well done," he said, "defending the chief of staff like that. You've saved your kneecaps this time."

Although Mac Stiofain had said on behalf of the Army Council that the military campaign would continue, we realized that the speed with which he had made his announcement had been unfortunate, as it gave the impression that the Provisionals had not given any thought to the proposals and were simply trigger-happy. It was reported in the press too that the Belfast Provisionals had wanted to call a temporary halt, and it was partly in deference to their wishes that a lull in the campaign was decided upon. In particular, we realized, any more civilian casualties like those of Donegall Street would have a very bad effect on public opinion when it was thought that the British government had made a substantial concession to our views. But against this there was the constant fear of appearing weak —particularly in the face of a mammoth two-day strike of Loyalist workers, organized throughout the Six Counties by William Craig, that took place throughout the Six Counties on the Monday and Tuesday following the British government's announcement. Several "peace" campaigns began, organized by women in Derry and Belfast. They were seized upon eagerly by the press as representing the wishes of ordinary people in defiance of the tyrannical IRA; we considered them middle-class and called them the "peace at any cost brigade." On April 2, Easter Sunday, Sean Mac Stiofain travelled into Derry to give an Easter oration (the rest of us went to different parts of the country to give orations: Joe Cahill to Cork, Dave to Mon-

aghan, I to Leitrim, while Ruairi stayed in Dublin). Mac Stiofain's oration assumed the most importance, in view of the Derry
women's movement, and he said that to accept the Whitelaw
proposals would be a compromise that betrayed the men and
women who died for freedom in 1916. Direct action against the
Belfast women's campaign was taken the following day, when
the formidable Republican Maire Drumm led a detachment of
Provisional women into their meeting and wrecked it. On April
6 an Army Council meeting was held which cemented over the
cracks in the movement that had appeared briefly on the day of
Direct Rule. Afterwards Mac Stiofain declared that the only
road to peace lay through the British government's accepting
the movement's three-point peace plan, put forward before the
three day truce of March 10

A day later, Whitelaw released seventy-three internees, the
first to be freed since Direct Rule. We had feared again that
their release would remove one of the Catholic population's
grievances and that our support would soften as a result. Our
fears were misplaced; we soon discovered that men who have
been held in prison without trial for six months do not forget
the experience quickly. We also found that many of the men released were coming home with a far greater political consciousness than when they had been arrested. In Long Kesh, of
course, there was nothing to do but talk (although many men
carved mementos of their stay—harps, plaques, rifles, even
Thompsons—out of materials their families brought in for
them).

There had been a three-day discussion of regional government, we learned; and we heard of increasing interest in Sinn
Fein in the Six Counties, even though it was an illegal organization there. I also met two ex-internees from Derry who had
decided to learn Irish, and they asked me to get hold of some
textbooks for them. "Would you be sure they have the fanatic
alphabet?" they asked me—so that they would know how to
pronounce the words. On April 13, the military campaign was

renewed in earnest, with fifteen bombs exploding across the Six Counties. Two days later Joe McCann, a member of the Official IRA, was shot down by British troops as he tried to escape in the Catholic Market area of Belfast. A dramatic photograph of him kneeling with an M1 carbine against a background of flames, taken during a street battle in Belfast in August 1971, had already become one of the movement's icons; and his life story, and the nature of his death, quickly became one of the myths of Irish Republican history. The Officials played the myth for all it was worth, with a massive funeral procession and a funeral oration given in Belfast at great personal risk by Cathal Goulding. Although McCann was an Official, the incident was another which brought us a new wave of emotional support and added confidence with which to carry on the campaign. The day after the funeral Lord Widgery, Lord Chief Justice of England, published his findings on the killings of the thirteen men of Derry who died on Bloody Sunday. I must admit that even we were amazed at the tortuous lengths he had gone to to avoid drawing the conclusion that seemed to us inevitable, even on the basis of the evidence contained in his own report. He said that some paratroopers' firing had "bordered on the reckless"; he found that there was "no evidence" that any of the thirteen who died had been shot while handling a firearm or bomb; and yet he contrived to exonerate the Army from any blame for what had happened, saying that the senior officers had been "sincere" in their intentions and that there was "no severe breakdown in discipline" among the soldiers. To the people of the Twenty-six Counties, his report confirmed what they already knew: that you couldn't trust the British.

# 11

# New Republican
# Myths

*"What does it matter
if Protestants get killed?"*

Like the Officials, we were quite ready to play for all they were
worth the new Republican myths that were being created out of
the current campaign. And nowhere was it easier to capitalize
on them than in the United States, where whole communities of
Irish-Americans were watching the struggle in the Six Counties
like spectators at a morality play, with right and wrong, good
and evil, delineated in black and white. It was in the United
States that our main fund-raising efforts were conducted, and
the visiting speakers, who included Ruairi and John Kelly, the
Dublin arms-trial man, were carefully briefed as to how the
audience should be played. There should be copious references
to the martyrs of 1916 and 1920–1922, the period most of the
audience would be living in. Anti-British sentiment, recalling
Cromwell, the potato famine, and the Black and Tans, could be
profitably exploited. By no means should anything be said
against the Catholic Church. And all references to socialism
should be strictly avoided; tell them by all means that the Ireland we were fighting for would be free and united, but say
nothing about just what form the new free and united Ireland
would take.

The formula was, in general, very successful; and how easy it was to raise money in the United States is shown by what happened when Billy Kelly went there.

I first met Billy Kelly—the brother of John Kelly—soon after I had joined the Provisionals, when I was in Monaghan for one of the regional government meetings. I knew of him as another of the legendary figures of the movement—I still believed in legends at that time—whom Ruairi himself had trained during the 1957–1962 campaign. In June 1970 he had taken part in one of the Provisionals' first military actions, the battle of Saint Matthew's Church in the small Catholic enclave of Short Strand, across the River Lagan in predominantly Protestant East Belfast. Protestants attacked with sniper fire and gasoline bombs, and the battle lasted six hours before the British Army finally arrived. By then four Protestants were dead or dying, and two Provisionals were seriously injured, including Billy McKee, the Belfast commander.

I was in the Monaghan Hotel, where the regional government meeting was being held, when I met the Republican Labour MP in Stormont, Paddy Kennedy, at that time still closely involved with the Provisional movement. "Billy Kelly's downstairs," Kennedy told me. "He's feeling very bad. Would you ever go down?" I did, and saw a thin figure standing at the bar, motionless save for the movement of his elbow lifting a whisky glass to his lips. His eyes were staring fixedly at the back of the bar, and it was not hard to discern that he was very drunk. I introduced myself, and he said that he knew of me through his brother John. He continued to look ahead of him as he drank. That night Paddy Kennedy drove myself, a friend, and Billy Kelly back to Dublin. I sat in the front seat; Kelly lay sprawled unconscious across the back seat, his head nestling against my friend. He kept jerking convulsively, and his feet would shoot forward into the back of Kennedy's neck, so that Kennedy had to keep stopping to push Kelly's legs back down again. Kelly was, I realized, completely played out after taking part in the struggle in Belfast for over two years.

This was the man now going to speak on behalf of the Provisional movement in the United States, and in many ways he was a suitable representative of the "freedom fighters" of Belfast. He began by missing his plane to New York after a hard night's drinking. For a time we heard nothing, and then received a telegram telling us to get him home again. We heard later that as soon as he had had a few drinks he would begin touting for arms in a most unsubtle way, once giving a United States Senator a conspiratorial elbow in the ribs and muttering, "Any hardware?" The final outrage came at a meeting where Kelly had said that the Catholic Church had caused a great deal of trouble in Ireland. Afterwards a middle-aged Irish-American lady had approached Kelly and asked him, "Excuse me, but did I hear you say something against the Catholic Church?" "Fuck off," said Kelly loudly. In total silence, he walked out. But despite these incidents, Kelly's fund-raising was no less successful than anyone else's.

We also received money from other revolutionary groups in Europe, of whom several came to visit us in Kevin Street. But they were mostly rather unconvincing people: the only ones who were of real use to us were the Basque resistance groups, who traded fifty revolvers in return for training in the use of explosives. (These were the negotiations which Mac Stiofain interrupted with his perverse inquiry as to whether the interpreter could speak Irish.) Most pathetic of all was an Italian who came to see us, wanting to join the IRA. He met Ruairi and Dave, who quickly passed him on to me. He persisted that he wanted to enlist, and I told him that the movement couldn't use him—he couldn't even speak English. All right then, he said, but could we teach him how to make bombs? He wanted to start a campaign of urban guerrilla warfare in Italy; he intended to wreck the life of Rome, he said. I passed him to Paddy Ryan and said that Paddy would use him if he could. I'm sure Paddy couldn't. We had other visitors from Palestine and from the Breton resistance movement, but all they seemed to want was to express their solidarity with us. We didn't want their sympathy; we were only interested in concrete help.

The military campaign was vital, and we knew as we achieved success after success that the British would have to talk to us. But when Mac Stiofain came into the Kevin Street office one morning and announced, "We've got to have a policy," it was for him a change of emphasis indeed.

For it was in readiness for negotiations that Dave, Sean, and Ruairi O Bradaigh had been working at the movement's political campaign throughout the previous year. For a long time the word "politics" itself had been a dirty one to the movement. Politics meant compromise, sell-out: the sell-out of 1921, when one faction of Sinn Fein had signed the treaty with the British which accepted the partition of Ireland; the sell-out of 1927, when Eamonn de Valera, who had led the Sinn Fein faction which refused to accept the treaty, then took his supporters back into the Irish Parliament. To persuade the Republican movement that "politics" meant otherwise was proving a hard struggle; and for Mac Stiofain to suppose that the movement would suddenly adopt any policy that the Army Council handed down to it was fantasy indeed.

None the less the Army Council decided it would spend some £500 on buying literature from Sinn Fein, who were amazed when the sudden order came through. The pamphlets, about Sinn Fein's economic policy and the idea of regional government, were loaded into a car and taken into the Six Counties, where the Provisionals opened offices and displayed the pamphlets for sale. But in the Six Counties there was no tradition of politics at all; at least in the Twenty-six Counties the Republicans knew their political myths. For a long time, of course, the Catholic population of the Six Counties had been disillusioned with the entire political process, a feeling going back to the cynical gerrymander of which the country had been born.

The men joining the IRA since 1969 had done so out of the

desire to defend their houses and their streets from attack. Some came from Republican families, but many joined the movement simply as soldiers. Sinn Fein had undoubtedly suffered, too, as a result of being declared illegal in the Six Counties. But on the other hand the movement did gain political depth from internment itself, which gave many of our members the opportunity to spend hours and days discussing politics.

But an opportunity presented itself for the movement to conduct a concerted political campaign on one specific issue. On May 10 Lynch was to hold a referendum on whether Ireland should join the European Common Market in 1973. Lynch's party, Fianna Fail, was supported over the Common Market by the so-called opposition party, Fine Gael. We were opposed to the Common Market, because it represented a rationalization of existing economic structures within Europe and would further cement Ireland's economic ties with Britain; once Ireland was in, we considered, the possibility of change within would lessen rather than grow. We decided that we would campaign against entry, asking people to vote "No" to the question whether Ireland should join.

The Army Council held a meeting which Dave missed because he was ill; afterwards Ruairi telephoned him and congratulated him, ironically, on being appointed director of the Common Market campaign, to be conducted in the name of Sinn Fein. Despite Ruairi's sarcasm, Dave did welcome the campaign as an opportunity to communicate the movement's policy, especially on regional government. It would also test, and develop, Sinn Fein's organization throughout the Twenty-six Counties, and attract new members.

But the EEC campaign would have a still wider significance. It would establish the Provisional movement as a serious political presence. We knew now that the British government would have to talk with us; and we assumed that information about our political position was already being passed on to it by the ever-widening range of politicians with whom we were in contact. Before Christmas we exchanged opinions, through interme- diaries, with the two Protestant leaders Ian Paisley and Des- mond Boal. At the time of the Civil Rights campaign, Paisley had been considered an extreme Protestant, but he had since become more moderate. He had consistently opposed intern- ment, and in November he had given an interview in which he said that Protestants would look at the Twenty-six Counties "in a different light" if alterations in Ireland's 1937 Constitution, guaranteeing the Roman Catholic Church's "special place" in the state, were made. Ironically at around the same time six Conservative MPs from Westminster had arranged to meet Ruairi and Dave as part of a fact-finding tour through Ireland. Ruairi was actually getting ready for the meeting, sorting through the literature he wanted to give them, when he read in the Dublin *Evening Herald* that it had been cancelled. We learned later that the MPs had been summoned by Maudling, then still British Home Secretary, and Whitelaw, then leader of the House of Commons, and told that on no account could they talk to terrorists. To complete the irony, four days later Mau- dling completely ruled out the possibility that there would be Direct Rule by Westminster of the Six Counties.

But now we were having increasing meetings with two main groups: the SDLP members, principally John Hume and Paddy Devlin; and a group of professional men and businessmen from Dublin and Belfast who called themselves Conciliation Ireland. Mostly former pupils of a grammar school in Omagh in the Six Counties, they had started as a group opposed to internment after a colleague had found himself in Long Kesh, but they had then broadened their campaign to try to organize a conference on the future of Ireland. They met Lord Grey, Governor of the Six Counties, and Lord Windlesham, Whitelaw's Minister of State. They talked mostly with Dave O'Connell, and gradually the conditions on which we might agree to suspend military ac- tivities emerged. One bone of contention was what such a halt might be called. We always resisted the term "cease-fire," which to us meant a one-sided declaration that we would cease operations; we wanted a genuine truce, agreed by both sides, and with a previous acceptance of some of our conditions by the British as a guarantee of their good faith. We had a deep distrust of the British, with every reason, after internment and the Compton report, Bloody Sunday and the Widgery report. Then there had been our three-day pause in March, used by the British Army to pick up thirty-three of our men. Mac Stiofain, for one, did not relax his customary precautions, as shown by an incident around this time which involved the SDLP MPs Paddy Devlin and Ivan Cooper. Devlin and Cooper visited Mac Stiofain at his home in Navan to discuss Provisional policy. They were in the habit of carrying automatic pistols, which was admittedly sensible in their positions. But Mac Stiofain had them frisked in the hall before they were allowed to see him, and their arms were taken from them.

Mac Stiofain's attitude towards another politician further demonstrated his inherent distrust of the established political process. Frank McManus, the Westminster MP who had been very sympathetic to the Republican movement and who had even succeeded Paddy Kennedy as chairman of the committee formed at Monaghan in August 1971 to explore the possibility of a new Ulster assembly, called at Mac Stiofain's home. But because McManus had taken his seat at Westminster, the heart of British dominance over Ireland, Mac Stiofain refused to see him. Later that day McManus, who was accompanied by his brother, called at the Kevin Street office. Ruairi was there and asked them in for a chat. He didn't realize at first that Mac Stiofain had refused to see McManus; when McManus told him, Ruairi just laughed.

Another politician we met, both before and after Direct Rule was introduced, was the Independent Unionist MP at Stormont, Thomas Caldwell. We realized that Caldwell was probably out to make political capital from meeting us—what a triumph it would be for him to persuade us to agree to a cease-fire—but thought it worth while once again explaining our position. He met Ruairi alone, and then myself and Ruairi on an occasion after Direct Rule. But all he wanted was that the fighting should stop. He wanted us to call a cease-fire and had no conception that we had even limited political demands that would have to be met first. "If only you knew how depressed poor Willie is," I remember him saying—it was representative of his level of argument—"waking up every morning to hear there's been a new explosion. Why don't you give him a chance?"

But despite these futile encounters, and the displays of intransigence by Mac Stiofain—the negotiating was conducted principally by Dave anyway—the Army Council felt it increasingly urgent that it should reach some form of agreement with Whitelaw. The talk was no longer of the risk of a Loyalist "backlash," but of the apparent dangers of out-and-out civil war, and nothing demonstrated the apparent slide into chaos better than the events of the third week in May. It was the week too when my own doubts about the Provisionals' operations surfaced for the first time.

On May 13, a car-bomb exploded outside Kelly's Bar, a Catholic pub at the junction of the Springfield and Whiterock Roads in Belfast. It was crowded with men watching the soccer match between England and West Germany on colour television, and after the explosion, in which some men were injured, shots were fired at the survivors from the Springmartin Estate, a Protestant housing area. Volunteers from both the Provisionals and the Officials joined forces to return the fire, using Thompson sub-machine guns, M1 carbines, and even a Bren gun. The battle lasted well into the night, and at the end of it three Catholics and a British soldier had been killed. The Army tried to say that the explosion had been a Provisional accident, but our volunteers would not have taken the risk of taking such a large amount of explosives anywhere near such a crowded bar. The Catholics of Belfast were sure a bomb had been placed by the UDA. The following day a young Catholic was shot dead as he walked along the Protestant Shankhill Road; on Monday a car-bomb exploded without warning outside the Protestant Bluebell Bar, injuring fourteen people.

On Wednesday, May 17, came an incident which in its implication and aftermath was to me the most serious of all. Some members of the Belfast Fianna boys—the junior IRA—fired rifles at Protestant workers going home from Mackie's, an engineering factory in the Springfield Road, and injured four of them. We knew of rumours that arms were being manufactured at Mackie's for the UDA, and I later heard that a team from the BBC TV programme *24 Hours* had actually filmed a Mackie's sub-machine gun—some Provos had captured it from Loyalists—being test-fired in the Twenty-six Counties. (The film was never released.) But in that case, the correct action would have been to blow the factory up (several attempts had in fact been made). The goal of the Provisional IRA was a new Ireland; how did you move towards such a goal by firing on Protestant workers?

The day of the shooting was my mother's birthday, and my family had all gone out together to a pub with entertainment provided by Irish ballad-singers. Ruairi and Joe Cahill were with us too. We did not return home until 3:00 A.M. and heard only a brief news item about the shooting which was difficult to make sense of. In the morning we read some more details in the newspapers, and RTE asked Ruairi to answer questions about it in a radio interview.

This put Ruairi in a difficult position, for he did not consider the shooting justified. Nor did he have any information to help him excuse it. He appeared on RTE—a little jaded from the previous night's celebrations, it should be added—and told the interviewer that he couldn't justify or explain what had happened.

The interview drove Mac Stiofain to fury. He telephoned Ruairi and screamed at him, "You must stand by the people in the North. How dare you say you don't know the circumstances?" Ruairi was angered not only that Mac Stiofain should rant at him, but also that he appeared to be saying that Dublin had to justify, retrospectively if necessary, every action Belfast took.

But how could the shooting of unarmed Protestants be justified? I wondered. Instead of trying to pull away from the threat of sectarian civil war, here was the movement taking us even nearer to it, and apparently justifying its actions only in terms of retributive retaliation—the politics of the most recent atrocity, it has been called. And I now recalled the angry discussion that had followed a recent car-bomb incident which had killed several civilians. "What does it matter if Protestants get killed" Mac Stiofain had raged. "They're all bigots, aren't they?" This had shocked both Ruairi and Joe. Ruairi's mother came from Belfast, and Joe's wife still maintained their home in the Falls Road, travelling down to Dublin regularly to see him. "She could be walking past the next bomb to go off," Joe had said quietly. And what a change had taken place in Mac Stiofain's outlook since the early days of the campaign, when two policemen in a rural area of the Six Counties had been blown up. Ruairi had spent nearly two days trying to calm him down and reassure him. "They were just country cops," Mac Stiofain kept saying. "What will their wives do?"

Following the Mackie's shooting, Ruairi, Dave, and I, agreed in our opposition to Mac Stiofain's actions and attitudes, now discussed, quite seriously, whether it would be best for the movement if Mac Stiofain were assassinated. There was no moral objection to this at all, said Ruairi; British soldiers were killed as the movement's enemies, and this Mac Stiofain had now become. But the major objection he raised was the effect assassination could have on the movement itself. There was the danger of a breakaway by the Six Counties, or at least by some units fighting there, particularly in Belfast, where Mac Stiofain had been assiduously building his power base. Old-guard Republicans such as Billy McKee and Francis Card, with whom

Mac Stiofain was not popular, had been arrested; and Mac Stiofain took careful personal interest in the new Belfast men who came to Dublin. He had a principal ally in Seamus Twomey, Belfast's commander since Joe came south after internment.

Assassination, too, would show our enemies that we were divided, one thing which we were always quick to deny—even when it was true. ("Absolutely no question of a split at all," I used to tell inquisitive reporters after speculation of a split had appeared—even though I knew behind the scenes strong rivalries were being played out.) But principally we saw that the main hope of forestalling civil conflict lay with the negotiations now gathering momentum, and the apparently sectarian incidents that followed Mackie's made it even more important that they should succeed. In succession, sixteen people were injured by a bomb in a Protestant area; a forty-six-year-old Catholic man, father of six, was found shot dead; so too was a fifteen-year-old Protestant boy; two Catholic teenagers were machine-gunned from a passing car as they stood in a queue in a fish-and-chip shop; and then fifteen Protestant children were taken to hospital with shock after gunmen had directed fire towards them in the Protestant Roden Street. That weekend the UDA erected its first barricades throughout Belfast, and several Catholic families living behind the barricades had their homes wrecked.

But even though the pressure for a truce was on, we were determined as always that we would negotiate from strength; since the start of the bombing campaign in 1970 we had caused damage in the Six Counties costing nearly £40,000,000. In the fourth week of May—the week following the incident at Mackie's—the Belfast brigade intensified its operations, with three or four bombings a day, including several gelignite bombs of a hundred pounds or more. We had before us the example of the Officials, whose campaign petered out over the same period, following another crass misjudgement by them. On May 20 they had tried and executed a nineteen-year-old Roman Catholic, William Best, a soldier serving with the Irish Rangers, a British infantry regiment in Germany. Ranger Best's home was in Derry, and he had come home on leave; Irish regiments of the British Army never served in the Six Counties. He was well known in the community, and that week had taken part in such traditional Derry pastimes as throwing stones at British Saracens and attending the wake of a Catholic youth who had been shot by a British soldier. His death—he was blindfolded and shot in the back of the head on a piece of waste ground— enraged many of the local population and gave new impetus to the Derry women campaigning for peace, who saw Whitelaw four days later. On May 29 the Officials declared a cease-fire because, they said, of "the growing danger of sectarian conflict." We shared their fears, but we knew that the Officials' declaration had been made from a position of complete weakness. After the cease-fire many young Official activists joined the ranks of the Provisionals.

But now another factor had to be weighed amidst the pressures on the Army Council at that time: the ever-shifting attitude of the Lynch government towards us. A number of Republicans were in Mountjoy prison, having been charged or convicted of illegally possessing weapons and ammunition, or similar offences. But Martin Meehan and the other Belfast men arrested after the big border incident of January had all been released; so too had the Dublin Official IRA leaders taken in after Aldershot. On May 10 Lynch's referendum on the Common Market was held. The result was 1,042,000 yes, 212,000 no. Dave and I laughed when we saw the figures; with the Dail's governing and opposition parties united against us, it was hard to take the referendum seriously as a test of public opinion. We had known that we had not a chance of winning, but we were pleased all the same at the interest our campaign had aroused in many areas of the Twenty-six Counties. We attracted many new young people to Sinn Fein—although sadly the party did little to hold their interest afterwards. Nor did we consider the referendum a fair test, for it was worded without presenting voters with any alternative to the Common Market. Our own alternative, a democratic socialist government organized on regional lines, was too hypothetical for the voters to take seriously. The bread-and-butter issues predominated. How much would food prices rise? How much could a farmer sell his bullock for?

But after the result was announced, Lynch did not merely say that the referendum meant that the people of Ireland were united in their desire to enter the Common Market; he also had the quite breathtaking nerve to say—or to allow it to be said for him, in well-placed leaks in the Dublin press—that the size of the majority gave him a mandate to act against the IRA.

On May 18 there was a serious riot in Mountjoy by the Republican prisoners, in which one wing was almost totally wrecked. This gave Lynch the opportunity to bring in an emergency bill enabling civilian prisoners to be transferred to military custody. The Curragh camp, where IRA men had been interned in previous campaigns, was readied to receive a new generation of Republican prisoners. On May 26 special courts were set up in Dublin under the 1939 Offences Against the State Act, with three judges reaching verdicts without a jury. In the movement we knew very well that this was a preparation for moving against Provisional leaders. It was stating the obvious when Ruairi told me, "Any one of us could be arrested."

But Lynch's move could not have come at a worse time—not simply for us, but for the prospects of a truce across the Six Counties. For this was the time when negotiations with the British were really intensifying. For months, we assumed, Lynch had been under pressure from the British government to move against us; and when he did so, his action not only jeopardized the negotiations but also strengthened Mac Stiofain's position on the Army Council at the expense of Ruairi and Joe —and, indirectly, Dave.

# 12

# Truce

*. . . the last British soldier*
*had been shot.*

I was at home on May 31, when Ruairi telephoned from Roscommon to say that Joe Cahill had been arrested in Kevin Street that afternoon; Ruairi knew that the police and the Special Branch would be coming for him too, as a police officer had been round to tell him so. Ruairi thought he was being given the chance to escape, but he decided not to take it. "How could I, as President of Sinn Fein?" he asked. "I wouldn't be any use to anyone on the run."

At 5:30 I heard confirmation of Joe's arrest on the radio, and then there was a news flash to say that Ruairi's house was "under siege" by the police. I rang at once; a policeman answered. He wouldn't let me speak to Ruairi, but Ruairi's wife came to the phone. "He's been arrested," she said.

I found it hard to credit that, of all the members of the Provisionals, Lynch should decide to arrest Ruairi. Joe Cahill was an IRA figure in the public's eye, and therefore a natural target. But Ruairi had been consistently put forward as a moderate, someone capable of seeing both sides of a question. Lynch's action was bound to hinder our negotiations, and we could imagine the British government's reaction. Lynch must have been asking himself, "Can't I do anything right?"

It seemed that if Joe and Ruairi had been arrested, then any member of the Provisionals could be at risk, including myself. The only course of action open to us was to demonstrate with such vehemence outside the Bridewell prison, where Joe was held, that Lynch would recoil from any further arrests. I went quickly down to Kevin Street; apart from the Sinn Fein Treasurer, Tony Ruane, the office was empty. I assumed that the demonstration had already started. "Where is it?" I asked. "Who's speaking?" Tony replied. "Nothing has been arranged."

I hurried down to the Bridewell, about ten minutes' brisk walk from Kevin Street. I expected to find some kind of gathering; just one person was there, Sean O Bradaigh. It was a disillusioning moment. Despite all our attempts to politicize the movement, only two people had realized that the only possible reaction to the arrests was to come out on the street and demonstrate. Sean and I hurried back to Kevin Street and started telephoning as many Sinn Fein supporters as we could. By nine that evening we had mustered about ninety people, just enough for a presentable protest. We paraded outside the Bridewell with placards, and then Sean and I addressed the crowd. But it was all too polite and too peaceful. I remembered the fighting in Ballyshannon, County Donegal, just before Christmas, when three Republicans had been arrested over incidents on the border; and the rioting that had taken place in Monaghan in March after three more Republican arrests, when the crowd had felled trees and barricaded a police station to prevent Irish troops from relieving its besieged occupants. That was what was needed in Dublin that night, I thought. With our dull, sparsely-attended meeting we were giving Lynch a completely free hand. In the morning police arrested Sean O Bradaigh at his home in Glengeary.

There were also warrants for Dave and Mac Stiofain, we read in the press, although this was never confirmed to us. They did go on the run—but it seemed strange that if the Dublin police had really wanted Dave they allowed him to go into the

Kevin Street office five minutes after Joe had been arrested and then spend half an hour there. (Ironically Dave and Joe had been due to meet the American religious leader Billy Graham.) Dave also spent a good deal of the subsequent ten days in a flat in the Ballsbridge area of Dublin, and Mac Stiofain visited it too. It would have been quite easy to trace them there by following me, for I visited them both frequently.

When Lynch had first set up the special courts, Ruairi discussed with Sean and Dave the action they might take if they were arrested. They decided on a hunger strike, one of the great emotional weapons of the Republican movement. In 1920 the Mayor of Cork, Terence MacSwiney, died in Brixton jail after a hunger strike that lasted seventy-five days. In 1940 the IRA men Tony D'Arcy and Jack McNeela died in Mountjoy, D'Arcy after forty-two days, McNeela after fifty. I remember speaking at Sinn Fein meetings where the mere mention of their names was enough to raise a loud cheer. Before he was arrested, Sean invoked their spirit by declaring, "I'll not eat their food, drink their water, or sleep on their beds."

But Sean, I had come to think, was very idealistic; I remember when we drafted the statement on the result of the Common Market referendum he wanted to include the words: "The Irish people will reject the materialistic values of the EEC." This, I thought, was fair enough as a piece of rhetoric; but then I discovered that Sean actually believed it. Unlike Joe and Ruairi, veterans of jails such as Mountjoy, Crumlin Road, and the Curragh, Sean had never been inside before. He was not, as he once admitted to Dave, a physically brave man—he had said that he did not have enough courage to join the IRA. He was treated badly on his first day in Mountjoy; when he asked for some water the warder who brought it for him deliberately kicked the glass over. He was under pressure from his wife, who was very concerned about him while he was in prison; and he had more to lose than the others, because unlike Joe and Ruairi he had not given up his job to work for the movement full-time and worked as a training officer for CIE, the Irish State transport company.

Ruairi suffered too, even though he had known from experience what prison entailed. He had wondered if he was fit enough to stand up to a hunger strike, as he was overweight and had ulcers too. (It seemed to be a fashionable ailment amongst the Provisionals; Dave and I both had ulcers as well.)

In the hospital wing of Mountjoy he dreamed of meals at Joe's Steak House and would be on the verge of plunging his fork into a juicy piece of beef, only to wake up. In reality, all he and the others took was a cup of warm water four times a day. With their increasing hunger, Ruairi and Sean both suffered from the cold and wrote asking us to send in football jerseys and socks for them to wear. Joe, although now fifty-two, seemed to take prison in his stride, having been on hunger strike before. He gave the others advice, telling them that the hunger pangs and nightmares of the first few days would pass. He suggested that they write out their defences for their court hearings as soon as they could—before their eyesight was affected. They also found they became very emotional, crying readily, and Joe told them this was another effect of the hunger strike. It was during the strike that Sinn Fein asked me to become its director of publicity—the post previously formally occupied by Sean, although under the pressure of events the division between people's roles in Kevin Street was frequently blurred. In that period I met Dave most nights in the flat he was staying at while he was supposed to be on the run.

On June 2 we issued a statement saying that the movement would continue with "the final decisive battle in the long fight for Irish freedom," and declared that "the secret talks which had been going on over the previous six months with Northern groups would cease." These talks, we said, could have led to an all-Ireland conference, but they would not be resumed while the Offences Against the State Act was being used against us. The statement was aimed directly at Lynch, accusing him by implication of wrecking the chances of a truce in the Six Counties. (On the same day we also claimed responsibility for one of the more interesting explosions of the Belfast campaign: on May 30 a bomb had gone off inside a policeman's locker in the Springfield Road RUC station and military post, and one soldier had been killed. It would have been a remarkable feat to have taken the bomb in past police and Army guards, and later I heard it said that the gelignite which exploded had been stored in a locker by a policeman who had seized it during an explosives raid and intended to give or sell it to the UDA; maybe it was one of the rare occasions when our claim of responsibility was based more on hope than on fact.)

On June 6 I went to Roscommon for Ruairi's first appearance in court. He had been driven the seventy miles there from Mountjoy in handcuffs for a hearing which we all knew would be a charade. One of the charges against him was of possessing "incriminating documents," including a copy of the five-point peace plan of September 1971. (Later, demonstrators waving copies of the peace plan paraded outside Lynch's suburban semi-detached in Rathgar, Dublin, inviting him to have them arrested too.) There were several hundred sympathizers outside the Roscommon court, and when I walked in, the hearing was already in progress. Looking around, I saw that Ruairi was opening his mouth and speaking, but although he was one of the movement's most powerful orators, I could not hear his voice. He looked drawn, his skin was yellow, and his hands were trembling; a week on hunger strike had already had a visible effect. He was remanded again without any evidence being presented against him, because the police said they had not yet completed their inquiries. Everyone knew there were no inquiries to complete. Two days later Sean O Bradaigh was released from the Dublin Bridewell, after the state had offered no evidence at the Central Criminal Court. He cried when Republican sympathizers congratulated him as he walked out. At the same hearing, Joe Cahill was remanded again, this time to the

Special Criminal Court itself—the first of the Provisional leaders to whom this happened.

Back in Dublin, I met Dave again to discuss the hunger strike and the effect Lynch's action was having on the chance of a truce. There was no question of talking, Dave still insisted, while Ruairi and Joe were still in prison. But I was rather shocked by Dave's apparent lack of interest in how Ruairi was suffering. It was fundamental that the movement was led by a coalition, but when I protested that no one seemed to want him or Joe out, Dave told me, "You're getting emotionally involved."

But even more surprising was Dave's attitude towards a decisive move Mac Stiofain had made to strengthen his position on the Army Council. It was customary when Army Council members had been arrested in the past to wait for their trial and possible sentence before deciding whether to replace them. But now that Ruairi and Joe had been arrested, Mac Stiofain moved with conspicuous haste to fill their places. The Council voted that their positions should be taken by Seamus Twomey, commander of the Belfast brigade and a staunch Mac Stiofain man; and by Sean Keenan, a former leader of the Derry Provisionals who had just been released from Long Kesh, whose allegiances were less clear.

But Dave didn't seem concerned at Mac Stiofain's obvious power ploy, partly as a result, I think, of the continuing estrangement between Dave and Ruairi, following my affair with Dave. But partly Dave was preoccupied by his encounters with John Hume, Stormont MP for the Foyle constituency of Derry, who was a busy intermediary between the Provisionals and Whitelaw. Dave was speaking again of moving on to a "new plane." (It was a phrase he used when his enthusiasm for a newly discovered idea was at its strongest, as when he decided that if he made me pregnant his wife could look after the baby and there would exist a totally harmonious relationship between the three of us.)

In meeting Hume, Dave was delighted at being able to discuss politics with someone who was his intellectual equal, and it flattered him to be treated as such by a well-known and established politician. I think he was a little seduced by the notion of political power and by the feeling of being at the centre of the decision-making process. With a different background and start in life, I'm sure he could have been a successful politician within the system. But when Dave told me that he was actually considering an alliance with Hume, perhaps taking part of the Republican movement with him, I thought he was moving into the realm of fantasy. Hume had consistently supported the Catholics of the Six Counties, but at the same time condemning violence, and it seemed clear to me that he was considering an alliance with Dave only to broaden the basis of his power within the SDLP, where there was continual jockeying for position, and within the Catholic population of the Six Counties as a whole. It was quite unrealistic for Dave to suppose that any sizeable section of the Republican movement would have gone with him, for there was still total distrust of the SDLP and its attempts to capitalize on the achievements of the Provisionals.

Dave's attitude towards both the hunger strikers and Ruairi was a revelation to me and markedly affected my feelings towards him. Our attraction for each other had a large intellectual element, from the moment when we discovered we shared the same political interests and attitudes. But I thought that to contemplate an alliance with Hume was suicidal—and more than that, I thought he had sold Ruairi out. It was really the end of my affair with Dave, and another fragment contributing to my incipient disillusionment with the movement.

But my determination to work for the movement then, and for the truce that seemed to be nearing, was not affected. We spent some time that week preparing advertisements for Dublin's two Sunday papers, the *Press* and the *Independent,* protesting at Ruairi's and Joe's continued imprisonment and presenting the facts of their hunger strike. The Army Council had decided these would be worth the £2000 to £3000 they would cost, and both newspapers verbally accepted our order. The *Press* accepted it formally too, and took our money; but the *Independent* refused to confirm the order, and half an hour later the *Press* phoned to say it had changed its mind. Its advertising manager would give no reason, and we were convinced that the Lynch government had put pressure on the two papers to refuse.

The Sunday in question was Wolfe Tone Day, when the father of Irish Republicanism is honoured by all political groups, from the governing Fianna Fail to the Official and Provisional IRA. Our meeting at Wolfe Tone's grave in Bodenstown, County Kildare, was attended by our biggest crowd in years. I spent much of the day with Dave in the Dublin hideout: we were depressed at finding the flat devoid of drink and were unable to go to a bar because Dave was nominally still on the run. We went to a friend's flat instead, and Dave said optimistically that his "policy" of not continuing negotiations would result in the release of Ruairi and Joe, and then talks would resume.

On June 13 Mac Stiofain held a press conference at the Brandywell Community Centre, a gloomy hall in the Bogside area of Free Derry; Dave, Seamus Twomey, and Martin McGuinness, commander of the Derry Provisionals, were there too, another defiant gesture against the British security forces. The purpose of the press conference was to offer the British a truce. But the offer was made in very different terms from those of March. Mac Stiofain said that if Whitelaw agreed to talk with the Provisionals, they would suspend "all offensive military operations" for seven days, provided that the British Army ended arrests, searches, raids, and "harassment of the civilian population." The big changes were that the Provisionals were no longer insisting on the ending of internment, or on any major policy declaration by the British, before a truce could be called. At the same time, the Provisionals once again emphasized their military strength, with a dozen bombs across the Six Counties on June 12 and 13, including one which devastated Derry's Victorian Guildhall. (Ten days earlier Derry's City Hotel, the most popular hotel for journalists, was closed after being wrecked by a bomb. The story is true that it had been spared by the Derry brigade for a long time because a friend of one of the Provos worked there as a night porter. But then he was sacked; two weeks later the Derry Provos blew the hotel up.)

On the same day that we made our truce offer from Derry, Whitelaw rejected it. It has been written that the SDLP was the first to perceive the significance of the Provisionals' drastically modified position, and that it then approached Whitelaw and pointed out to him that we were no longer making impossible demands about internment and British declarations on the future of Ireland. This version of what happened supposes that our modified offer was totally ingenuous; in fact we made it as a result of an understanding we had reached with Whitelaw through our negotiating contacts. Although Whitelaw publicly rejected our offer, we knew he had to do that; afterwards our contacts with him in fact intensified, at first through intermediaries, then directly by telephone between Dave and Whitelaw himself. (Whitelaw's later denials that he had negotiated directly with the Provisionals before the truce referred only to face-to-face meetings.) We were aware ourselves that our own move to hold talks could have been considered a betrayal by our supporters. Ruairi was released from prison on June 13, and although Dave was convinced this was a victory for his "policy," Ruairi told me he thought he'd have been let out anyway. But Joe Cahill was still in jail—and here was Mac Stiofain offering to talk to Whitelaw. Dave at this time was very edgy and said that we knew if anything went wrong—as he felt it so easily could—he could be the movement's scapegoat. "I'll be shot," he told me.

The day after Ruairi was released I called at his house in Roscommon. I was to convey to him the news that he had been replaced on the Army Council. (He remained, of course, president of Sinn Fein.) He just didn't believe me. "You're overwrought," he responded. "You're under strain and you've been working too hard. My friends wouldn't do this to me." It was impossible for me to convince him that my news was true, but later other people confirmed it to him. The news plunged him into a deep depression and delayed his recovery from the hunger strike. When Joe was finally released a week later, after nineteen days on hunger strike, Ruairi went to tell him that he too no longer had a place. He took it more philosophically than had Ruairi; but there was no doubt that the faction opposing Mac Stiofain had received a serious blow, and that Dave was going to find himself increasingly isolated.

Sean Mac Stiofain was also becoming increasingly apprehensive at this time, both about the dealings with Whitelaw and about the manoeuvrings on the Army Council. Possibly he feared a counterstrike by Dave O'Connell, who was now at the centre of the intensive political activity going on. I spent several days with Ruairi after his release and on June 17 went with him to a meeting in Longford. We were back quite late, and at 2:30 in the morning there was a phone call from Mac Stiofain.

There had been yet another speculative newspaper story that there was a split in the Provisional leadership and that Mac Stiofain was about to hand over control to Dave O'Connell. He insisted that I put out a statement denying it at once, which I duly did, phoning it over to RTE in Dublin at 3:30 a.m. Ruairi and I agreed that for him to become so agitated about such a flimsy story—one of the many that appeared with unfailing regularity—showed that he must have been feeling very nervous, not to say insecure. (Mac Stiofain betrayed his own anxieties to me a short while later, saying that he thought the rumour had done "more harm to Dave" than to himself. "I had phone calls and letters from all over the country," he added. "People rallied to me.")

The dealing between ourselves and Whitelaw was becoming more subtle. Dave now asked him for a gesture of British sincerity: would he meet the demands of the Republican prisoners in Crumlin Road jail, Belfast, to be granted political status? Whitelaw had good reason to agree, for the former Belfast commander, Billy McKee, had been on hunger strike for a month, and on June 13 a rumour had swept Belfast that he had died. The strength of Catholic feeling was shown by the fact that in the afternoon a dozen buses and lorries were hi-jacked and set on fire all over the city. Whitelaw went a long way towards what Dave asked. He said that "prisoners serving sentences for certain offences" could have separate accommodation, could wear civilian clothes, and would be subject to less discipline. Dave accepted his compromise as meeting the spirit of the Provisionals' request. Even so, the path towards a truce remained delicate, fraught with the possibility of misunderstanding. Whitelaw issued his instructions on the evening of June 18, but there was a delay in passing them on to the jail itself, his officials apparently not realizing the precarious nature of the deal being worked out and that the death of Billy McKee would have ruined everything. Whitelaw's orders eventually reached the jail in the early hours of June 19.

We knew that an agreement was near when Joe Cahill was released from prison in Dublin on June 20, the special court dismissing the charges against him. He had been on hunger strike for nineteen days but seemed astonishingly fit when he came out. By this time, too, Whitelaw had ordered the release of more than five hundred internees and detainees; 370 remained.

I went out with friends on the night of Wednesday, June 21, and drank a lot, arriving home at breakfast time. At 10:30 the phone rang; it was Dave. He told me that he was driving up to Donegal that day to see Deirdre, who had been complaining of not being well; would I go round to the hideout flat to see Mac Stiofain? I said I would, and I was getting ready to go out when

Mac Stiofain himself phoned. He was very agitated and asked me to come round at once. When I arrived, he had a statement ready for me, offering the British a bilateral truce—there was the usual careful avoidance of the term "cease-fire"—on just one condition. "The IRA," said the statement, "will suspend offensive operations provided that a public reciprocal response is forthcoming from the Armed Forces of the British Crown." The statement was handwritten, and I recognized Ruairi's writing, but I didn't comment on this, as I knew I too was supposed to maintain the fiction that as President of Sinn Fein he was not involved in the Provisionals' activities. (When I saw Ruairi alone later I said, "I see you've been writing out statements." "Bitch," he said.)

The reason why Mac Stiofain was so anxious there should be no delay became clear: on a pre-arranged schedule, our statement was to be issued at 2:00 p.m. I went round to the Kevin Street office and phoned it over to the Press Association, the three broadcasting stations, RTE, BBC, and UTV—the Six Counties' commercial television channel—and the Dublin newspapers. Then I went back to the flat.

Mac Stiofain by now was very nervous indeed, pacing back and forth in the flat, occasionally sitting down uneasily and munching biscuits from a packet on the table. The Provisionals' statement had already been broadcast, and he was waiting for Whitelaw's agreed response. His fear was that Whitelaw would renege on the deal; he listened to all the news broadcasts, flipping the tuning switch on the transistor radio from one station to another. "It hasn't come across yet," he kept saying. But a BBC man had told me that Whitelaw would not begin to speak in the House of Commons until later that afternoon and that there would be no news until 5:00 or 5:30. Telling Mac Stiofain this didn't appear to help him relax. Then we heard the news: Whitelaw had accepted the truce with the words "If offensive operations by the IRA in Northern Ireland cease on Monday night Her Majesty's Forces will obviously reciprocate." Mac Stiofain had his statement responding to Whitelaw's reply all ready, and I hurried back to Kevin Street to phone it through. It was longer than the first one, and said, "We take Mr. Whitelaw's words as meaning that he accepts our request for a reciprocal response from the British Forces and accordingly the cease-fire will begin at midnight on Monday." It was an hour or more before I was back in the flat once again.

Mac Stiofain was a changed man, actually smiling and obviously feeling expansive. He first wanted some fish and chips —his favourite meal—to celebrate, but the fish-and-chip shop hadn't yet opened. He told me what a good job I'd done that day, and I hadn't got over the surprise of hearing him compliment me when he asked me out to dinner. I was amazed; never before had he shown such interest in me. I said I didn't think that was a good idea because I thought we might be recognized —even now, of course, he was still in theory on the run. Then I took a gentle rise out of him, saying, "But of course you're very good at disguises." I was referring to a Hitler-style moustache he had grown and been photographed in at the Derry press conference on Tuesday. He thought I was serious and said earnestly that he hadn't liked the photographs published of him afterwards and had decided to shave it off. Then he actually made a very hesitant pass at me, putting his arm round me and asking if I would stay there with him. I suppressed a shudder and left. I was feeling shattered, after the previous night's drinking and today's tensions, and was ready for sleep.

Reactions to the news of the truce were as expected: the Unionists, from Faulkner down, were predictably vicious as the prospects of an end to their fifty-year dominance became real. The British government had made a deal with the Provisional IRA, sworn and mortal enemies of Stormont, and to the Unionists this was the final betrayal of the partnership between themselves and the British Conservatives. The truce had come, Faulkner said, 453 murders too late—a clear implication that everyone who had died in the Six Counties had been shot by the IRA, including the thirteen who died in Derry on Bloody Sunday, Seamus Cusack and Desmond Beattie, and Joe McCann. We had expected the Loyalists' fury, but we did not know then how far they would go in their efforts to wreck the truce. In the coming fortnight we were to find out.

On June 23, Seamus Twomey announced in Belfast that any Provisional breaking the truce would be executed. But the truce itself was timed to begin at midnight of June 26 and 27, and we had no intention of de-escalating our activities until then, as this would once again allow people to suppose we had negotiated from weakness, not strength. The British Army was to call our operations from June 22 to June 27 the Six-Day War, and in that period six soldiers died and at least a dozen were wounded. Two minutes from midnight a soldier was shot dead from the Short Strand area of Belfast. People I knew outside the movement were to tell me it was a "pity" he had died so near to safety, but in our eyes a truce was a truce, and it began at the time agreed. Until then, British soldiers were a justifiable target, as they always had been. They knew why they were there, and so did we; our volunteers' attitude was "kill or be killed."

I spent the evening before the truce was to take effect with Dave; still very sentimental, he had said he wanted us to be together at midnight, the moment when all his hopes about the movement would culminate. The movement had fought a campaign over three years which had now achieved recognition of the Provisionals as a political force, with legitimate demands that the British government recognized. The key understanding we had with Whitelaw, Dave explained, was that we would have a place at a conference on the future of Ireland. In the nearer future, we believed, internment would end, and British forces would withdraw from Catholic areas. The truce was not a compromise, but a point from which we could only progress. In the totally fluid situation Ireland was now in, we felt that all things were possible.

We waited for midnight over a meal in Joe's Steak House; Dave was certainly quietly exhilarated at what he had achieved and began to see himself as above the sordid politicking of the Army Council. It had been agreed that Mac Stiofain and Dave would be in the team that would negotiate with Whitelaw, together with Twomey, Martin McGuinness, Gerry Adams, an internee whose release Whitelaw had ordered so that he could take part, and Ivor Bell, a Belfast staff member. But there was no place for Ruairi, and he was feeling hurt at this. But he found no ally now in Dave. "I'm not taking any sides in this," he told Ruairi. Dave was ordering bottle after bottle of white wine; Ruairi, still suffering from ulcers, sat disconsolately drinking milk. Outside it was pouring with rain. We heard the news soon after midnight that the last British soldier had been shot from Short Strand; it made the point, we felt, that we could continue to operate in Belfast even when the British Army was at its most alert. Then, after midnight, all actions ceased. The truce was a reality. It was Dave, I think, who said it: "We've done it."

# 13

# A Position
# of Strength

*. . . we intended . . . to use the truce*
*to advance our scheme of Eire Nua.*

On Tuesday morning the truce was reality. The furious fusillade which occupied the final moments of Monday night died abruptly on the stroke of midnight. In the Catholic area of Andersonstown, a Belfast Provisional stronghold, Twomey was directing the truce together with Mac Stiofain himself, who had driven up from Dublin to join him. From Dublin, we issued a statement saying that the action before midnight showed "that the IRA is far stronger and better equipped than it has ever been before." We added that the Provisionals "would stand on full alert to take defensive action should the need arise and ready to resume offensive action if the leadership decide that is necessary." I was very busy on Tuesday in Dublin, for we had called a press conference for Wednesday, when we intended to explain our position and to use the truce to advance our scheme of Eire Nua. This was a further development of the regional government scheme for Ulster presented at Monaghan in September, and included plans for a new constitution for Ireland. The old constitutions of the Six and the Twenty-six Counties would be abandoned; there would be a central government with separate assemblies for the four old provinces: Connaught, Munster, and Leinster, as well as Ulster. We had prepared a glossy pamphlet with a colour cover, printed on good-quality paper, with a map showing the four proposed regional areas. The assembly governing the four provinces could pass laws permitting divorce and contraception, if it wished.

It took me all Tuesday and much of Wednesday to telephone all the newspapers we wanted to invite to the press conference, to ensure that all our nominated representatives would be there, and to confirm the arrangements with Dublin's Ormond Hotel, where the conference was to be held. Originally, the press conference was to have been conducted in the name of Sinn Fein; but on Wednesday Mac Stiofain phoned through from Belfast to say that he wanted it under the banner of the Republican movement. Ruairi had been going to act as chairman, but now Dave replaced him. Ruairi was disappointed at this and saw the move as another by Mac Stiofain to reduce his influence; but the move would help establish that it was the Provisionals who were speaking at the press conference in the wake of the truce and their implied acceptance by the British government as a political force. The Belfast Republicans Maire and Jimmy Drumm, and Sean Loughran, a Belfast Provisional officer, would be there—it was important that the policy should be seen to come from members of the movement from all Thirty-two Counties—so too was Paddy Ryan, the Army Council member who had been at the forefront of the burning of the British Embassy. The line-up was strongly IRA—to have called it a Sinn Fein occasion would have stretched the meaning of the words even further than usual.

There was a degree of risk involved in holding the conference at all, for Dave was still supposed to be on the run, and it would be his first public appearance since the arrests of Joe, Ruairi, and Sean. The conference was to start at 3:30, and as we arrived we recognized the familiar faces of the Dublin Special Branch; they made some attempt to look more trendy than ordinary police, wearing coloured shirts and with their hair touching their shirt collars, but they were still very obviously policemen. They were taking their usual copious notes of everything that happened, but made no move to arrest Dave or any of the other speakers. Several I knew were even quite friendly. "Hello Maria," said one. "How are you getting on?"

The press conference seemed to go well, with what seemed a genuine interest in the audience to discover what our scheme involved, but there was some persistent questioning over any change in divorce and contraceptive laws. Ruairi replied consistently that the individual would be free under law to do as he wished. But one reporter said rather pointedly, "Mr. O'Connell seems to be very silent on this point." Dave said, with his customary poker face, "It would be a private matter of individual conscience."

There was a shock for us after the meeting when we learned that there had been a warning of a bomb in the hotel; all the staff had been evacuated and waited outside on the pavement. But nobody, it seems, told us, and the conference went ahead in blithe ignorance. Afterwards I sat in the hotel lounge, drinking tea with Dave and Ruairi while the Special Branch took photographs of us together through the window.

The press conference had been successful, but afterwards I began to feel more doubts about the course the movement was taking. I was disturbed, first, on Ruairi's behalf. He had been trying to recover his place on the Army Council in the most direct manner possible—simply by still attending at the meeting places and forcing Mac Stiofain into asking him to leave. (Eventually his persistence paid off, and he was reinstated.) He had also been working hard with several lawyers on the nuances of the policy and the statement of intent that were to be presented at the coming meeting with Whitelaw, due to be held on Friday of the following week; but even so, he was still not to be included in the team who would see Whitelaw. His shaky position indicated to me that the coalition of interests and personalities on which the movement had depended was reaching breaking-point, and that Mac Stiofain was dominating the movement more and more. He was not a man, I thought, with whom the movement could be trusted.

And as each day of the truce passed, the news from Belfast became more and more disturbing, with a number of apparently motiveless killings of civilians. The first two who died were Catholics; they were followed by three Protestants, then three more Catholics, then three Protestants again. What was happening? It was hard to escape the conclusion that here was a retaliatory series of sectarian murders. Had we underestimated the determination of the Loyalists to wreck the truce? It was, of course, in their interests to destroy the accommodation the British government had come to with the Provisionals, to demonstrate that any attempt at reaching agreement with us was bound to fail. No one was more outraged at the agreement than the militant UDA, by now making martial noises with as much ferocity as it could work up. We thought it most likely that it was behind the killings of the Catholics, unhindered by the British Army. But clearly, too, some members of the Republican movement were retaliating in the same senseless way, and the slide into outright sectarian warfare seemed to be continuing. This could wreck the position we had reached. How much would the Catholic population tolerate? How long would they hold to the truce, and would they consider our own attempts to make a deal with the British a sell-out? Would a new "Catholic Army" or the "Provisional Provisionals" emerge, beyond Dublin's control? Would it have been better to have imposed a time-limit on the truce, so that the Catholics would have had a target to aim for? With all these considerations and worries, it seemed ever more urgent to reach a really concrete agreement.

Dave was still optimistic about the progress of negotiations, however; he told me that he trusted Whitelaw and admired him as a politician—and it was indeed a remarkable achievement

for a politician raised in the remote and gentle world of Westminster to come to grips with the military realities of politics in
the Six Counties. He and Dave seemed to be forming a mutual
admiration society; scarcely a day passed without a statement
appearing in the press as to how highly they esteemed each other's abilities. Dave had agreed to a gesture of good faith on the
Provisionals' side which would also help Whitelaw meet pressure from the Loyalists; on June 30 three of the smaller barricades on the edge of Free Derry were dismantled—although, as
Dave pointed out to me, "the most important ones would remain." The gesture evidently satisfied Whitelaw, but not the
UDA; on the same day that the barricades were removed, it hijacked a number of Belfast buses in preparation for building its
own barricades the coming weekend.

On July 2 a Loyalist leader, Gusty Spence, disappeared
while he was on a weekend's parole from Crumlin Road jail.
He had been imprisoned in 1967 for murdering a Catholic bar-
man, and when he disappeared several newspapers speculated
that he had been kidnapped by the IRA for revenge. Of course,
he hadn't—there was nothing we could do with him—and we
realized very well that he had gone into hiding with one of the
militant Loyalist groups and would take a part in the sectarian
war, should it come. The next day there was a major confrontation between the British Army and the UDA over barricades
erected in Ainsworth Avenue, Belfast. The British were apparently taking the attitude that if the UDA wanted to barricade
its own areas and cause itself inconvenience, that was all right;
but in this case there were Catholic families within the area the
UDA wanted to enclose, and on previous weekends Catholics
in similar positions had had their homes wrecked. There were
tense negotiations at street level, with consultations with Whitelaw himself, and at the end it seemed to us that the British
Army had gone too far in accommodating the UDA; we knew
this would again leave the Belfast Catholics uneasy.

There was a full-scale meeting with Whitelaw on July 7; this time Dave flew to England with Mac Stiofain, Twomey, McGuinness, Ivor Bell, and Gerry Adams. When I saw Dave afterwards, he was once again pleased. "Things are going OK," he said. He thought that the chances of a lasting truce remained high, and there was to be another meeting with Whitelaw a week later. Out of this, he hoped, could come a definite statement by the British that the troops would be withdrawn by a particular date, and to meet this the Provisionals themselves would have to offer to declare their own end of hostilities. They would go in with an open mind, he said, to see what the British were really prepared to offer, and then thrash out their own position in the Army Council before returning to Whitelaw with their response. Although he remained hopeful, he was realistic enough to accept that the meeting with Whitelaw on June 21 could simply end in deadlock. But that the Provisionals would have a place at a conference on the future of Ireland had already been agreed. It was the high point of Dave's achievement, and I recalled the difficult course he had steered to reach it, beginning with having to persuade Mac Stiofain himself that it would be worth while talking to the British. Now, said Dave, they would be at the conference table, and they would take part in decisions that would be made about the future of Ireland. He was brimming with confidence, too, in his own ability to deal with people and began considering even talking to Lynch—"We'll try a direct approach," he said. At this point, I thought, he had taken off into fantasy again: some members of the movement disapproved of the Provisionals talking even to the SDLP, while to deal with the head of the Irish government and the leader of Fianna Fail would be disastrous. But there was no denying that Dave's achievement was already considerable, and that the IRA—Provisional or otherwise—was in the strongest position it had achieved in fifty years. Twenty-four hours later, that position had been lost.

# 14

# Conflict as
# Usual

*. . . political judgment was needed . . .*
*but all the Provisionals knew was to bomb.*

I had a telephone call at home on Sunday morning, July 9,
from Colin Smith, the *Observer* reporter who had interviewed
me just after I joined the Provisionals and who had written a
story naming me after Amsterdam. He had been wondering
whether to come to Dublin that day, but then he said he felt
there could be trouble in Belfast, and I agreed with him that
he'd do better to stay there.

At eleven Ruairi called for me; the Provisionals had helped
organize a demonstration that afternoon at the Curragh, where
the Republican prisoners convicted on arms charges or for belonging to the IRA, some by Lynch's special courts, were being
held (the same camp from which Ruairi and Dave had escaped
in 1958). Republicans were due down from the Six Counties,
as well as supporters of Civil Rights groups and left-wing organizations such as the Young Socialists. There was already a
fairly large crowd waiting to march to the camp when we arrived, and Ruairi and Joe Cahill briefed the marshals who were

to guide them. It was, they said, to be a peaceful demonstration; once again we did not want to provide Lynch with an excuse to act against us.

Then Ruairi and Joe went to see the camp commander to explain their intentions. At the gatehouse they met a Captain O'Neill, who complained, "I know nothing about any demonstration," and he refused to let Ruairi even send word in. One of our Special Branch acquaintances was hovering outside, and Ruairi asked him to explain to the obdurate captain who they were and what they wanted. "Sure, Ruairi," he said. Eventually Ruairi and Joe were face to face with the camp commander, who had been at the Curragh when Ruairi had escaped with Dave. "We know you," he said. "You were here before." "Yes," agreed Ruairi, "and I showed you a clean pair of heels." Ruairi explained to the commander that they intended to hold a demonstration which, Ruairi fully hoped, would be peaceful.

We realized that this hope could be a pious one when we saw the Belfast contingent. One was carrying a hurley stick, and they were clearly spoiling for a fight. Seeing them, we thought there was a strong chance that a serious confrontation might occur with the Irish Army—which a few weeks before had drawn bayonets to face demonstrators from the less militant Six Counties action group, People's Democracy. Not that such a confrontation would be against our interests; it would attract press and television coverage and would also crystallize the issues facing us: Armed Troops Repel Demonstrators at Republican Prison Camp, and so on. On the other hand, we did feel genuine sympathy for the young Irish troops, among some of whom we knew there was considerable Republican feeling. We heard that some of the Belfast men were armed, and the last thing we wanted was for an Irish soldier to be shot.

The march began, and as soon as the camp perimeter came into sight the Belfast contingent just broke ranks and ran, ignoring the vain shouts of "Keep calm" from the marshals. We saw police and troops running to head them off, and in no time demonstrators were drawn up facing a line of Irish troops. I saw an officer pulling a reluctant soldier into line; like many of them, he was obviously scared, as he had every right to be. Without any experience in riot control, he was facing men and women with three years of street fighting behind them.

We began the meeting from the back of our truck, although many of the demonstrators were ignoring us and concentrating on the troops. The Belfast Republican Maire Drumm did her best to keep emotions on the boil with a speech in which she called the troops "vermin" and "pathetic illiterate lackeys of Jack Lynch." Ruairi and Joe looked at each other, but it was too late to stop her. We could see sticks and bottles flying and smoke rising from a sports pavilion that the demonstrators had set on fire. Then, just as the meeting ended and people were drifting away, I saw demonstrators running across the grass; the Irish Army, for the first time in its history, had fired CS gas. Ruairi and I groped our way to Ruairi's car, skin smarting and eyes streaming. We saw the Westminster MP Frank McManus laughing at us from inside his own car. "Now you know what it's like in the Six Counties," he said.

Ruairi and I drove back to Dublin, and Ruairi came into my parents' house for a cup of tea and some brown bread. We turned on the television and were watching for news of the demonstration at the Curragh when the phone rang. It was a Dublin newspaper reporter, and he had an urgent piece of news which he wanted to check with us. The Belfast Provisionals had called him to say that the truce was over. Was it true?

I couldn't believe it myself; I told the reporter that I had heard nothing myself but would try to check. I went and asked Ruairi, but he had of course heard nothing either. I told the reporter that it was very unlikely—perhaps the report he had heard had been mischievous?

Five minutes later the same reporter rang back. They had just heard from Sean Mac Stiofain, he said; the truce was off.

In that case, I said, it must be true. I went to tell Ruairi. "Jesus Christ," he said.

Both Ruairi and I were very tired after the demonstration, and there seemed little we could do. I went to bed still feeling that the situation was not too serious and that if there had been a break in the truce it could probably be patched up again quite quickly. In the morning the newspapers were full of stories of what had happened. There had been a confrontation at Lenadoon in Belfast between the Catholics and the Army, and when I read the reports I admit that I suspected the truce had been sabotaged by Twomey or Mac Stiofain himself. Then Dave telephoned me and said he'd like to come over to discuss the statement that the Provisionals would issue about the incident. When he came, we went over just what had happened.

It was, said Dave, one of those confrontations where both sides had got into positions from which they could not back down. But there was no doubt that the Provisionals, led on Saturday and Sunday by Twomey, had been acting for the mass of working-class Catholic opinion in the area. The issue of which the whole incident turned was housing, one of the main issues of the civil rights campaign when it started in 1968. With the growing militancy of the UDA, Catholic families had been leaving mixed areas of Belfast during the previous two months, either because their homes had been wrecked or because they had been intimidated into moving out. June and July were traditionally the time when the Loyalists showed themselves; it was known as the "marching season," when parades of Orange bands went round almost nightly to collect money for the celebrations of July 12, the anniversary of the victory of King William of Orange, Protestant King Billy, at the Battle of the Boyne in 1690. For three weeks many of these families had been arriving in Andersonstown, a large postwar development to the southwest of Belfast, where they were put up on camp beds in a secondary school empty for the summer holidays. The most modern part of the development, where the confrontation

*Smithfield bus station in Belfast was one of twenty-six targets
bombed by the Provisionals on Bloody Friday*

Photograph by Topix, courtesy of the London *Sunday Times*

*Rescue workers lift a body into a polythene bag after a Bloody
Friday explosion wrecked Belfast's Oxford Street bus station*

Photograph courtesy of Press Association Photos

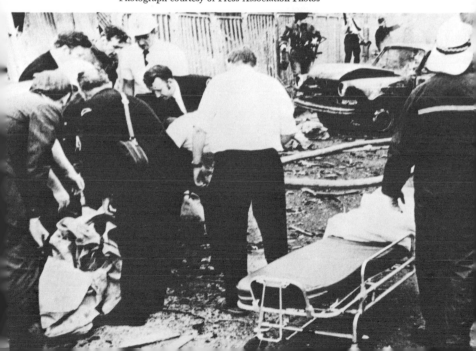

was to take place, was Lenadoon; with four-bedroom houses built in the mid-sixties, and much of it bordering on the countryside, it was potentially an attractive place, if it had not been the terrain on which a guerrilla war was being fought.

But adjoining Lenadoon was the Protestant development of Suffolk. On the edge of Suffolk, at the foot of Lenadoon Avenue, were some empty houses that Protestants had evacuated, whose windows and doors the Army had sealed with sheets of corrugated iron. The local UDA said that the Protestants who lived there had been intimidated into leaving by the Catholics. The Andersonstown Catholics replied that the Protestants had left of their own accord. The truth, as usual, was somewhere in the middle: the Protestants had moved out after being continually caught in the crossfire of nightly gun-battles between Provisionals and British Army patrols.

But the situation was that homeless Catholics were camped in classrooms, while good houses on the edge of a Catholic development were empty. There was considerable pressure on the Provisionals to act, and so the Andersonstown Relief Committee was formed. The committee started negotiations with the Northern Ireland Housing Executive to allow Catholics into the sixteen former Protestant homes. On July 6 the Housing Executive issued legal tenancies for five families, with the proviso that the British Army could decide when the families could move in, "in the light of the general security position in the area."

But this was too much for the UDA, and it decided to mount a show of force in the Suffolk area to demonstrate that there would be trouble if the Catholics moved in. Around midnight on Thursday, July 6, some two hundred UDA men practised their drill outside the disputed houses (some of the Catholics had already started to move their furniture in). This was enough for the British Army, which told the Catholics they couldn't move in because the Army couldn't guarantee their protection. The Andersonstown Relief Committee protested that this was UDA rule, and if the British Army couldn't protect the families, then the Provisionals would.

On Friday and Saturday the Provisionals organized demonstrations of local Catholics in Lenadoon Avenue; around three thousand people each day wound down the hill towards the houses, then turned back again. At the head of the procession was a tipper truck loaded with a family's furniture; behind came boys with hurley sticks and dustbin lids, followed by men carrying gardening and mechanics' tools, and behind them were women and children.

The demonstrations were an impressive but disciplined show of Catholic strength and feeling while negotiations were going on over the houses among Whitelaw's office, the Housing Executive, the British Army, the UDA, and the Provisionals (still calling themselves the Andersonstown Relief Committee). Twomey joined these negotiations on Saturday, going straight to Andersonstown from Belfast airport after returning from the Friday meeting in Britain with Whitelaw; Dave O'Connell, who had been at the Whitelaw meeting too, came to Dublin and stayed in touch with Twomey by telephone throughout that weekend. Twomey was in a bad temper even before he arrived in Andersonstown, his car having been stopped and searched by the British Army en route—"a clear breach of the truce" he told Dave angrily. The talks by now were taking place in the British Army post in Lenadoon Avenue, a heavily sandbagged row of three terraced houses known to the locals as Fort Newry, which was under almost continuous attack by the Provos throughout 1972; once they even tried to blow it up by ramming it with a mechanical digger with a gelignite bomb in the scoop. General Harry Tuzo, commander of the British troops in the Six Counties, took part in the talks in Fort Newry —though without ever meeting Twomey face to face—but by Sunday morning deadlock had been reached. Twomey gave the British a deadline of 4:00 p.m. to allow the homeless Catholics to move in, but the British did not budge.

There had been a third demonstration that day, with the same personnel, and at 5:15, the driver of the tipper truck, still laden with furniture, took action of his own, speeding off down Lenadoon Avenue towards the barbed wire, guarded by soldiers, which sealed off the disputed houses; the whole contingent of men, women, and children followed. Twomey and several of his officers caught up with the crowd and managed to pacify them while last-minute negotiations with a British Army major took place across the barbed wire. The Catholic crowd was angered at seeing several Loyalists on the Army's side of the wire, including one who actually had a Luger pistol tucked in his belt.

Then the talks broke off, with angry words from the British major; Twomey and his men walked off in disgust. Now the tipper truck tried to drive through the barbed wire. But it was rammed by a British Army six-wheeled Saracen armoured car and driven back into a second truck loaded with furniture, behind. The truck-driver was trapped in his cab, and the driver of the tipper was clubbed by soldiers as he tried to get away. A volley of rubber bullets scattered many of the demonstrators; some hurled broken paving stones at the troops, who replied with more rubber bullets. Some demonstrators were carried off with broken ribs or red, mushy faces from direct hits. Gradually the crowd fell back up Lenadoon Avenue and then turned its attention to Fort Newry. After showering it with stones and bottles, it started to uproot the protective wire-mesh fence, whereupon the garrison inside replied with CS gas.

It was at this point that the Provisionals decided enough was enough and that they would open fire. As clouds of CS gas drifted over the area, they started clearing Lenadoon Avenue of people. It was half an hour before they succeeded, and the British had ample warning of what was coming. Three volunteers opened fire with armalites and an M1 carbine from the ground floor of a block of flats. Firing lasted all night, but although hundreds of rounds were fired from both sides, there were amazingly no gunshot casualties in Lenadoon. In the rest of Belfast, though, as the Provisionals took up arms again, six soldiers were wounded, and six civilians, none of them Provisionals, were killed.

It seemed to me then that the Provisionals could not have prevented the breakdown of the truce, and I certainly didn't think that Twomey had been at fault. Possibly the unresolved conflicts had been too great. Whitelaw had been under pressure from the Loyalists not to come to any accommodation with the IRA; and while the truce was in operation, the British Army had not come to terms with the problem of the UDA. Catholic families in Protestant areas of Belfast were still being driven from their homes, which had led directly to the confrontation at Lenadoon. And the Catholic population's anger had keen kept at a high level by the murders of individual Catholics, seized or shot down in the street, of which there had been half a dozen or more. But even then the situation did not seem irrevocable. I was with Dave later that evening in the Royal Dublin Hotel, and he was very pleased at a statement Whitelaw had made in the House of Commons that afternoon. Whitelaw's version of what had happened in Lenadoon was quite dispassionate, and later leaks to the press confirmed Dave's opinion that Whitelaw had "left the door open." The problem was how to get back into negotiations again; Dave thought they could be resumed in a week or so's time.

But in the meantime the Army Council was preparing its own response to the breakdown. It met early that week and decided on a policy of retaliation for what had happened; there was no doubt in its mind that the British had betrayed it— Twomey made this clear publicly on July 13, when he told a journalist that if there was to be another truce the principal demand of the British would be "a pledge to keep their word." The spirit of that council meeting was that Whitelaw had to be shown that the Provisionals did not take this kind of treatment. The council also felt it needed once again to achieve a position of strength—as always, the basic position from which to negotiate, if negotiations were to be resumed. And not to retaliate, the council thought, would enable Whitelaw to ignore us and negotiate with the SDLP—as always, looking to take over our role as representatives of the embattled Catholics of the Six Counties. The principal target was the British Army, and within a week of the ending of the truce, twelve British soldiers had been killed.

But the Army Council's policy of getting back to the negotiating table through an offensive campaign failed. It failed, first of all, because the council no longer had control over Belfast. To its decree that the British Army was the main target it had added the rider that civilian casualties were to be avoided at all costs. But the day after the truce had ended there had been the six people killed in the crossfire of the Provisionals' battles with the British, including a girl of thirteen and a Catholic priest aged sixty giving last rites to a dying fifteen-year-old boy. The man who had been most aggrieved by what happened on July 13, and the most intransigent afterwards, was Seamus Twomey. And now the poverty of thought within the Belfast command was revealed. All along it had believed—as I had—that by terrorizing the civilian population you increased their desire for peace and blackmailed the British government into negotiating. But now it seemed Belfast could not deviate from its course. A political judgment was needed which would determine the nature of the Provisionals' selective response; but all the Provisionals knew was to bomb. A gigantic car-bomb wrecked Skipper Street in the centre of Belfast; five people were injured by another car-bomb in Lombard Street. Out of Belfast, too, Derry suffered an onslaught; and the shopping centre at the small town of Kilrea was devastated.

The importance of the political campaign Dave had been trying to develop over the past year was never more clear. In Belfast the movement had become a purely military one. The young men joining it were principally soldiers, fighting men, whom the Provisionals could use so long as Dublin remained in control. But as they acquired battle experience they had begun to feel that they should be making the decisions, not Dublin; they were on the ground, they knew the battleground and the people. For many of them, fighting had become a way of life. If we had managed to politicize them, there would have been a basis for unity between Dublin and Belfast, and the chain of command might have held. But we had not.

As each day of fighting passed, Dave realized that the possibility of returning to a position from which negotiations could be restarted was dwindling. He became very depressed, particularly as he realized he no longer had a role to play. In the weeks up to the truce he had negotiated with Whitelaw and secured a place for the Provisionals at a conference on the future of Ireland. He had been built up by the press, and respected by politicians for his negotiating skill—which was now of no use at all.

The vacuum he found himself in gave Mac Stiofain the perfect opportunity to assume full control of the movement. The Provisionals were once again conducting a military campaign —the only sort he knew. True, Belfast had been leading, Dublin backing it in retrospect; but Mac Stiofain now reasserted his leadership once again, taking the movement where Belfast wanted it to go.

I remember an incident which demonstrated how far the military campaign had developed its own momentum. Ruairi and I were in a car and in tuning in the radio we caught a newsflash from Belfast, hearing the figure "twelve"—another twelve civilians injured or dead, we wondered? What the hell had happened now? We recalled the time when we'd have known what was happening in Belfast without having to listen to a radio. In less than three weeks the movement had fallen back from the strongest political position it had ever achieved—the declaration of a truce—to one of total sterility. Dave knew it; Ruairi knew it; I knew it.

It was the end for me. I knew that there could be no hope of getting back to the high point of our campaign. We had used force selectively towards a goal which we had reached—and then lost. I could see no moral grounds left for continuing the military campaign. Maybe Mac Stiofain was imprisoned by the logic of his position and had no real choice before him. But I did not see why I should remain in the same trap.

I remained alone for several days, having no contact of any kind with the Republican movement. I wouldn't come to the phone, and after a while my family grew tired of telling lies on my behalf and just let it ring. I went out walking by myself, and once finished at Dun Laoghaire, the harbour five miles south of Dublin where the steamers sail for England. I walked out over the deserted piers and sat there for several hours, staring out to sea, my mind in a turmoil. I remembered why I had joined the Provisionals almost a year previously and what my objectives had been then. I did not accept that those objectives could be realized by the methods the Provisionals were now using. Was I really looking at it objectively, I wondered? Or was I too close to the people involved? Was I disenchanted with the movement because of the continuous power-play, and nothing else? But then I saw that the power-play itself was having a decisive effect on the campaign, as Mac Stiofain sought to confirm his position by using those very methods of which his rivals disapproved. I had been working for the Provisionals for eleven months without a break. A week previously, my friends in Madrid had suggested I go to stay with them for a holiday. I was decided: I would go to Spain.

# 15

# Disenchantment
# and Escape

*. . . almost for the first time,*
*I wondered about the crippled and the widowed. . . .*

The day before I was due to leave Ireland, Ruairi phoned, and
I said I'd like to see him. We met at the Ivanhoe Hotel, and
when I told him I was going to Spain the next day, he took the
news badly. He said there was too much for me to do in Dublin; he and Dave needed all the allies they could get, he pointed
out gently, adding that he thought there was still a chance of in-
fluencing the campaign. I couldn't tell whether he really believed that or not. I went through my objections to Mac
Stiofain and the way he was conducting the campaign, one by
one. I said I believed in revolution, in a new system of govern
ment in Ireland, and I could see no way that continuing the
bombing and running the risk of killing civilians could achieve
that. We talked for nearly three hours, and at the end he said
he agreed with me completely. But he said he was going to stay
in Dublin to continue the struggle for what he believed in. I
agreed, under pressure from Ruairi, that I wouldn't make a
final break with the movement. Ruairi said he was still hopeful
that he and Dave would be able to shake Mac Stiofain's hold

and effect a change of strategy. He suggested that I go away for two weeks, by which time the situation might have changed. I said that if it did change, I would return. Several days earlier I had covered half a dozen sheets of writing paper with the reasons why I was disillusioned with the movement, and when I told Ruairi this he said he'd like to read what I had written. I asked him to collect it from the house after I'd gone.

I stayed in Madrid for a while, then went south to Torremolinos. But, more than a thousand miles from Ireland, I couldn't stop wondering what was happening. All my friends seemed to be talking about Ireland too, but with very little grasp of what was involved; it became very wearing to keep explaining the issues from the basic historical principles. But there was no longer the unquestioning support for the IRA I had encountered in Spain a year previously. Too much had happened for that.

I was in Madrid when I heard about Bloody Friday. A friend came into the room and asked, "Have you heard about Belfast? There are eleven people dead." I asked, "Who? how? where?" But no one knew. I looked through the European newspapers but could form no clear picture of what had happened. I thought the whole situation had gone to pieces. I just couldn't see how eleven people could have died.

I stayed in Spain for another week, and in that time there were were several further incidents. Then came the news that the British were sending a further four thousand troops to the Six Counties, and the papers became full of speculation that there would be a major move against the Bogside and Creggan enclaves of Free Derry. It seemed that the Provisionals' military policy was now being matched by massive force, and that the chance of a negotiated settlement had finally receded. But I desperately had to know what was happening, and I couldn't face trying to unravel the confusion over a thousand-mile telephone conversation. I sent a telegram to Ruairi to tell him I was coming back.

Ruairi met me at Dublin airport. My first question to him was "What happened on Friday?" He simply replied, "There isn't anything to say." Then he told me that very day the British Army had gone into the Creggan and the Bogside in unprecedented force and that the Derry Provisionals had withdrawn rather than take on such overwhelming odds. The British, it now seemed, were committed to defeating the Provisionals by military means. After Ruairi told me this, we were almost silent as we drove up to the house. Then Ruairi gave me the most shattering news of all: Dave was off the Army Council and Ruairi was facing a court of inquiry. Instead of Ruairi and Dave joining forces to unseat Mac Stiofain, Mac Stiofain had strengthened his position still further. If I had been doubtful about the way the movement was led when I left for Spain, I knew now that there could be no hope at all.

Ruairi told me the painful details of how Mac Stiofain had asserted his grip even more firmly over the movement. First he told me about the court of inquiry he was facing. Although he had by sheer persistence managed to regain his seat on the Army Council, his hold had remained tenuous, and Mac Stiofain had taken advantage of this. The time and place of Army Council meetings were usually decided by the chief of staff, who would tell one member of the council where he should wait to be picked up and taken to the location. The word of the rendezvous would be passed on from member to member in turn; but on this occasion Mac Stiofain gave instructions that Ruairi was not to be told. But now, although he had known a meeting was in the offing, Ruairi assumed when no word came that the time had not yet been decided upon.

The council meeting was held without Ruairi, and Mac Stiofain produced a charge against him which meant there would have to be a court of inquiry—and also provided an excuse to displace him from the Army Council once again pending the result. While Ruairi had been on hunger strike, his wife had taken £50 from the float in Kevin Street to pay his telephone bill; it would certainly have been counterproductive if the president of Sinn Fein had no longer been available to talk to the world's press. But at the council meeting Mac Stiofain accused Ruairi of misappropriating funds and said that he should be court-martialled.

That evening Ruairi was in Kevin Street when Paddy Ryan came in and told him that he was to travel to Navan in the morning to see "the chief of staff." Why? Ruairi asked. Paddy Ryan told Ruairi in some embarrassment that there had been a council meeting that day and it had been decided that some action was to be taken against him—what it was, Paddy wouldn't specify.

The next day Ruairi drove the thirty miles to Navan and was shown into Mac Stiofain's room by his wife, Marie. Mac Stiofain was writing at his desk and for some moments did not look up. Then he picked up a document and showed it to Ruairi: it had Ruairi's name on it and the words "court-martial."

But Ruairi did not accept this as readily as Mac Stiofain must have hoped he would. "Wait a moment," he told Mac Stiofain. "There'll be no court-martial. I want a court of inquiry." (As following the Amsterdam affair, a court of inquiry would investigate all the circumstances of the incident and then decide whether a formal court-martial should be held.) The two men had a tense discussion, during which Ruairi said that he wanted an inquiry into why Mac Stiofain had not told him of the previous day's council meeting. Eventually, his hand shaking, Mac Stiofain crossed out "court-martial" on the document and wrote in "court of inquiry." The court, Ruairi said, was due to be held that Sunday, and it had been agreed that it would consider Ruairi's charge as well as Mac Stiofain's.

Then Ruairi told me the circumstances of Dave's deposition, which revealed once again the Machiavellian methods Mac Stiofain was prepared to employ against those he considered his enemies. While I was in Madrid, Mac Stiofain had declared at a council meeting that an interview Dave had given to a Dublin newspaper was "unauthorized." As a result, Dave was suspended not only from the Army Council but from the Provisional movement itself. That this punishment was ludicrous is shown by the fact that Seamus Twomey had given a very detailed interview to the German news magazine *Der Spiegel,* which led to a considerable storm in the British press and Parliament. But Twomey, being Mac Stiofain's ally, was merely "reproved," and no further action was taken. At the end of his suspension, which, I believe, was to last a month, Dave was to report to the commander of the Dublin Brigade for instructions.

I also learned that Mac Stiofain had written to the Ard Comhairle—the executive body—of Sinn Fein in connection with an interview I had given to *Hibernia,* a current-affairs periodical published fortnightly in Dublin. At the time, Sinn Fein had been rather distraught about the interview because I had dared to reveal that I was not a practising Catholic, and the Coiste Seasta—the inner committee composed of the Sinn Fein old guard of Ard Comhairle—had held its own inquiry, but its only conclusion was that Sean O Bradaigh should write to *Hibernia* as soon as he came out of prison to make it clear that the opinions quoted were my own and not necessarily those of the movement.

When this was learned by the Army Council, it seemed to regard it as funny, nothing more, and said little about it. But now Mac Stiofain had revived the whole issue, asking Sinn Fein that I be dismissed from the movement on the ground that I had held him up to public ridicule—this because of my stated opinion that the eyepatch he had been wearing since his eyebrow had been singed by a parcel-bomb was a "disaster." (My point had been that it gave the press too easy a target; we were trying not to look like a collection of thugs enamoured of violence.) It was indicative of the bad feeling then between Sinn Fein and Mac Stiofain that the Sinn Fein rejected his request out of hand, even though it did not have a high opinion of me either. I saw the whole trivial episode as another move by Mac

Stiofain to weaken the group opposing him. But it was far more serious that Ruairi was facing a court of inquiry and Dave had been deposed from the Army Council. Why, I wondered, had I bothered to come back?

Ruairi guessed what I was thinking and said I should make no final decisions until after the court of inquiry. He called me that Sunday evening around nine. "How did it go?" I asked. "Fairly well," he told me. He meant that both charges had been thrown out: Mac Stiofain's against him on the facts as they were presented; his against Mac Stiofain on the ground that he had no right to bring such a charge against the chief of staff after all. (Instead of waiting for weeks before giving its findings, as did the court following the Amsterdam affair, the court announced its decision that evening.) Ruairi told me that after the decision he came out of the sitting-room where all the witnesses, including Dave, had been waiting, and met Mac Stiofain in the hall. Mac Stiofain put out his hand, and Ruairi automatically shook it. "Here's to a better relationship," said Mac Stiofain.

The sincerity of Mac Stiofain's remark could be judged by what we heard Mac Stiofain was telling other people immediately after the inquiry. One of his techniques was character assassination by smear, and even though Mac Stiofain should not have discussed the proceedings of the court of inquiry, he was telling people that Ruairi had been "in a bit of trouble to do with money," but that the Provisionals had decided not to take any action against him, leaving the impression that it had been a magnanimous decision by Mac Stiofain rather than a judgment reached by the court itself. It was typical too of the movement that it should have worked itself into a state of righteous indignation over a charge involving money, when the morality of killing the people of Belfast seemed never to be worth examining.

In the week that followed I had several long conversations with both Dave and Ruairi; Ruairi was still saying that Mac

Stiofain could have been toppled if only they had stayed together at the crucial time. Dave was depressed at his own loss
of power and at the insulting requirement that he should report
to the Dublin command for instructions. Both he and Ruairi
still dwelt on the possibility of leading the movement back to
the position it had achieved at the point of the truce: could
there still be a way, even despite Bloody Friday and Whitelaw's
declaration that never again would he talk to the IRA? But I
believe they realized it was hopeless, that their chance had gone
forever. I remember going with Ruairi to see Sean McBride,
the former Irish government minister who had been a senior official of Amnesty International and had since become General
Secretary of the International Commission of Jurists, and he
said the same thing.

I also tried to find out just what had gone wrong on Bloody
Friday. What I had read in the press was that the Belfast Provisionals claimed to have given at least an hour's warning for
each bomb, but these warnings had not been followed up. But I
found it impossible to believe that no one in the Belfast leadership had realized how difficult it would be for the police and
Army to act on twenty or more warnings received in the space
of an hour. All along we had known that there were risks of civilian casualties due to misunderstandings of our warnings and
delays in acting on them. People had been killed, as in Donegall Street, when the authorities had only one bomb to deal
with. I could not avoid the conclusion that the probability of civilian casualties had been accepted, and perhaps even planned.
Whenever such casualties had occurred before, there had always been the pressure of events to take my mind off them. But
now, almost for the first time, I wondered about the crippled
and the widowed and the lives that had been changed forever.
Surely Belfast had realized how far they were overloading the
system, and that twenty warnings could never be dealt with? If
they hadn't realized it, they had no business dealing with bombs
at all. And if they had . . . There was no way their actions

could be justified. My suspicions about what had happened increased whenever I tried to ask in Dublin what had gone wrong. I met a blank refusal even to discuss it; for once there was no attempt to excuse, justify, expatiate.

Once again, I withdrew from Provisional activities, and when I met Dave and Ruairi we talked not about the future course of the movement but about my own doubts and worries. There was another Army Council meeting due to be held on August 23. The day before, I met Ruairi again, and he still maintained his optimistic line that it was possible to depose Mac Stiofain and reverse the movement's military policy. Ruairi said he would ring me afterwards to tell me what happened. He called me on the morning of August 24, a Wednesday. "Well?" I asked. "Er, well . . ." he said. It was enough to tell me that nothing had happened, that Mac Stiofain was still in control. Ruairi asked me if he could see me to talk about it some more. But I said I wasn't sure when I would be free.

The notion that I might one day write an account of my experiences with the Provisionals had been half formed in my mind for some time. I had occasionally made notes about my feelings, a few pages of which I had offered to Ruairi before I had left for Spain. I wrote some more in Spain and gradually became convinced that somebody must reveal, first to the rank-and-file membership of the movement, second to the general public, what was happening in the Provisional leadership. On an impulse, I scribbled a quick note to the *Observer* reporter Colin Smith and posted it to him from Madrid. In two recent conversations with him, the first when Ruairi and Joe were arrested, the second at the time of the Lenadoon incident, I had hinted at my dissatisfaction with Mac Stiofain and the military campaign. I addressed the note to Colin at the London office of the *Observer* and asked if we could meet as soon as possible.

But it was several weeks before he received the note. He had been in Belfast for a time and found it only when he returned to London. By then I was back in Dublin. He telephoned me at once and said he would be arriving at Dublin airport at 4:30 that evening. Could I meet him?

When we met he said at first that he had only an hour to spare, because he wanted to catch an evening train to Belfast. But he thought from my note that something was wrong; could I possibly be thinking of . . . ?

We drank a couple of glasses of white wine in the airport bar. I confirmed his suspicions and told him of the conclusions I had reached. He asked me if I wanted to go back to London with him and write my story for the *Observer*.

"But what about your train?" I asked.

"Oh, I think we might have to put that off for a while, don't you?"

I had not mentioned money, but he said that the *Observer* must pay me a fee for the story because I probably wouldn't be able to return to Ireland for a long time.

Now the decision was made, and there were several things to be done. I don't remember feeling any particular emotion at the time. I had always tried to discipline my feelings, and not to worry about events whose course I could not influence. Many defectors are no doubt a bundle of nerves from the moment they decide to cross sides. All I felt was relief that I was doing something positive after the weeks of talk, talk, talk, with nothing ever changing.

My biggest danger was from the man who undoubtedly had become my closest friend in the movement—Ruairi. I had hinted to him several times that, if nothing was done, I might just act on my own. If he discovered that I was missing he might put a watch on the airport straight away.

We decided that Colin should drive me back to my parents' house in Churchtown to pack. I would tell my mother that I was going away for a few days to try to sort things out in my mind; Colin would collect me in the morning, and we would leave Dublin on the first flight to London.

We drove back to Churchtown by a roundabout route; Colin

was still asking questions about what I might write, needing to be sure that I was going to be worth all the effort that would be involved. Evidently I convinced him; we stopped at a country bar, so that he could telephone several senior *Observer* staff members at home (it was by now well after office hours).

The village switchboard took a long time to call the numbers —and then nobody was in anyway. Colin rejoined me at the bar. As we finished our drinks John Kelly came in. It was an incredible coincidence, incredible bad luck. We were in a bar I had never visited before—and in walks a leading Provo. Although Kelly's status had waned since the Dublin Arms Trial, he was still financial director of Northern Aid, a fund-raising front organization for the Provisionals.

We greeted each other as if it was only natural that we should have met in that bar, and I could see that Colin Smith was looking wary, wondering if he hadn't been set up for something all along. I was sure that Kelly knew who he was—they had met at least once before, I remembered—so I introduced Colin by his own name, and we were soon discussing the latest moves by the SDLP. After half an hour, John Kelly left. I wondered whether the Provisionals wanted me to know I was being followed, but then decided that the chance meeting was innocent enough. I doubted whether John would tell anyone he had seen us that night; he saw little of the Provisional leadership any more.

Nevertheless, I decided to arm myself for the journey to the airport in the morning. Most Provisionals have weapons at hand because of the assassination risk, fearing not the UDA or even the British Special Air Services (SAS), the undercover group we knew to be operating in the Six Counties, but the nuts: the people who would send me newspaper pictures of myself with a neat hole marked in my forehead. I had two guns: an old but well-maintained Walther 7.65 automatic, and a newer revolver, which I didn't keep at home. Back in Churchtown, I removed the Walther from its latest hiding-place—

beneath a pile of washing—pulled off the tinfoil which kept if free of rust, and slipped it into my handbag.

At the airport the following morning I could see that Colin was fretting. He admitted that he was anxious about our passing through the Irish and British controls while I was armed. If I were caught with the Walther at Heathrow, the British Special Branch would have a holding charge on me right away.

We decided to dump it. I unloaded it and gave the magazine clip to Colin to get rid of. I wrapped the gun itself in a copy of the *Irish Times* and dropped it into a sanitary bin in a ladies' lavatory. Later I found that, in the scramble to catch the plane, Colin had not found anywhere to dispose of the clip; eventually, in Britain, he handed it over to the police.

Then came a final, anxious delay. The Aer Lingus captain announced that we would be a few minutes late taking off because several life-jackets had been stolen from under the seats on the previous flight. Colin was convinced that I had been seen dumping the Walther and that the airline was playing for time until the police came aboard. But then we took off, and over the Irish Sea I sipped black coffee and wondered what lay ahead. Ireland was behind me now.

# Epilogue

*. . . if I returned to Ireland*
*. . . I "could face execution."*

Ten days after I arrived in England, the first of my accounts of my time with the Provisionals and my disillusionment with the movement's campaign appeared in the *Observer*. It was followed by two further articles in successive weeks. Both they and this book have been aimed first of all at the great many honest and sincere members of the Republican movement who, I believe, have been quite unaware of the nature of the Provisional leadership. I wanted them to know what kind of man Mac Stiofain was, and I wanted them to realize the true reasons for the decisions he was making. If they then choose to continue in the movement, then that is their decision, but at least I have given them the chance to opt out for the same reasons that I did. I also want those who stay to know that the only hope for the Provisionals lies with men such as Dave O'Connell and Ruairi O Bradaigh, and not with men like Sean Mac Stiofain.

I also want to tell people who do not belong to the Republican movement but who feel drawn to it none the less, in Ireland, in Britain, in the United States, and in the rest of the world, just what it is they are supporting. I want them to know why the Provisionals have been killing soldiers and civilians in the Six Counties and wrecking the country's economy. If, once they know, they continue to support the movement, that again is their decision.

There are also those people who do not support the Republican movement, but who have followed the complex events in the Six Counties in various degrees of doubt and bewilderment. I want them to understand what the Provisional IRA has been fighting for, and where I think the movement took the wrong course. I want them to understand the motives of the many fine men in the movement—as well as the motives of men like Sean Mac Stiofain and those who think like him.

Of course I know that my account will be welcomed by the British as a propaganda victory in their fight against the IRA. As soon as I arrived in England, the *Observer*'s editor, David Astor, sent an emissary to see Whitelaw to find out what his attitude to the articles would be. He said that he was very pleased and was delighted that the *Observer* had taken him into its confidence. He arranged Special Branch cover for me, and the Special Branch sent word to me that there was no intention of holding me or interrogating me. I never met any member of the Special Branch, nor did I want to, but I felt that even to be in Britain with its tacit consent was an embarrassment and a compromise. It was a price I had to pay.

Soon after I arrived in England, I sent my parents a brief message, writing them a postcard which the *Observer* arranged to have posted in Paris. I just said that I was all right and would be in touch soon. Then, on the night before the first article appeared, I telephoned them from a London call-box. I had recorded interviews for both BBC and ITV, and I told them to watch for the late-night news bulletins, which would tell of my defection and the *Observer* articles. I just hoped all would become clear to them then.

Soon after midnight the Provisionals issued a statement in Dublin. It said that I had met Mac Stiofain on only four occasions and that I was "of little importance." I had, of course,

met Mac Stiofain dozens of times, and I thought that I would
have put out a more impressive knocking statement than that.

Later, Mac Stiofain said in an interview that if I returned to
Ireland the Provisionals would court-martial me and that I
"could face execution." I telephoned my mother again shortly
afterwards. We discussed what I had done, and then she said,
"There are very few places left for you now." That, I know, is
true.

# Chronology

## 1969

JANUARY 4
Civil Rights march attacked by Protestants
at Burntollet, near Derry.

APRIL 19
Riots as Derry RUC invade Catholic Bogside.

APRIL 28
Major James Chichester-Clark succeeds Captain Terence O'Neill
as Northern Ireland Prime Minister.

AUGUST 12–14
Siege of Bogside by Derry RUC.

AUGUST 14
British Army enters Derry.

AUGUST 14–15
Rioting in Belfast; ten civilians die.

AUGUST 15
British Army enters Belfast.

OCTOBER 10
B Specials (Protestant police auxiliaries) disbanded,
to be replaced by Ulster Defence Regiment (UDR).

NOVEMBER
IRA splits into "Official" and "Provisional" wings.

*Chronology*

# 1970

APRIL 1–2
Clashes between British Army
and Catholics of Ballymurphy Estate, Belfast.

JUNE 18
British General Election: Heath new Prime Minister.

JUNE 27
Catholic-Protestant clashes throughout Belfast.
Protestants shot in battle of Saint Matthew's Church.

JULY 2–5
British Army curfew in Falls Road district, Belfast.

# 1971

FEBRUARY 6
Gunner Curtis shot in Belfast, first British soldier to die.

MARCH 20
Chichester-Clark resigns; replaced by Brian Faulkner.

JULY 4–7
Rioting in Derry.

JULY 8
Seamus Cusack and Patrick Duffy shot in Derry.

JULY 15
SDLP MPs leave Stormont.

JULY
Maria McGuire joins Provisionals.

AUGUST 8
Renewed rioting in Belfast.

*Chronology*

AUGUST 9
Internment in Six Counties under Special Powers Act;
twelve die in street battles.

AUGUST 25
One killed, 35 injured, by bomb at Electricity Board, Belfast.

SEPTEMBER 5
Provisionals issue five-point peace plan, rejected by Stormont.

SEPTEMBER 6
Lynch and Heath meet at Chequers.

SEPTEMBER 27
Lynch, Heath, Faulkner at Chequers.

OCTOBER 11
British Army reveals plan to crater border roads.

OCTOBER 17
Czech arms for IRA discovered at Schiphol airport, Amsterdam;
David O'Connell, Maria McGuire go on run.

OCTOBER 24
O'Connell, McGuire, return to Ireland.

NOVEMBER 7
Ex-Home Affairs Minister William Craig
forms Ulster Vanguard movement.

NOVEMBER 16
Compton report confirms "ill-treatment" of detainees
by British Army. Seven men escape to Twenty-six Counties
from Crumlin Road jail, Belfast.

DECEMBER 2
Martin Meehan, Dutch Doherty, escape from Crumlin Road.

DECEMBER 12
Official IRA assassinates Senator John Barnhill.

*Chronology*

# 1972

JANUARY 17
Seven men escape from *Maidstone* prison ship in Belfast harbour.

JANUARY 27
Four-hour gun battle between Provisionals and British Army
across border in County Louth.

JANUARY 30
Bloody Sunday.
First Brigade of British Army paratroopers
shoot thirteen men dead in Derry
following civil rights demonstration.

FEBRUARY 2
British Embassy gutted in Dublin.

FEBRUARY 22
Seven killed by Official IRA bomb at Paras' HQ in Aldershot.

FEBRUARY 25
Officials shoot and seriously injure
Home Affairs Minister John Taylor.

MARCH 4
Two die, 100 injured, in explosion
in Belfast's Abercorn Restaurant;
Provisionals disclaim responsibility.

MARCH 10
Provisionals call three-day cease-fire in Six Counties.

MARCH 13
Harold Wilson begins visit to Dublin,
meets Lynch and Provisional IRA.

MARCH 20
Six killed by Provisional bomb in Donegall Street, Belfast.

# Chronology

British government announces suspension of Stormont;
Six Counties to be ruled directly from Westminster,
with William Whitelaw Secretary of State for Northern Ireland.

MARCH 27–28
Two-day strike of Loyalists, called by William Craig.

APRIL 19
Widgery Tribunal reports on Bloody Sunday.

MAY 10
Common Market referendum in Twenty-six Counties.

MAY 29
Official IRA announces cease-fire.

MAY 31
Joe Cahill, Ruairi O Bradaigh, arrested
under Twenty-six Counties' Offences Against the State Act.

JUNE 13
Provisionals offer talks with British.

JUNE 22
Provisionals agree on truce with British.

JUNE 26
The 102nd British soldier to die shot in Belfast,
two minutes before truce effective.

JULY 7
Whitelaw meets O'Connell, Mac Stiofain,
and other Provisional leaders in England.

JULY 9
Truce ends in clash with British Army
over Catholic housing in Lenadoon Estate, Belfast.

*Chronology*

### JULY 21
Bloody Friday.
Eleven civilians die as Provisionals
explode twenty bombs in Belfast.

### JULY 31
Operation Motorman: British Army enters Derry No-Go areas.

### AUGUST 20
Maria McGuire flies to London
with *Observer* reporter Colin Smith.

### SEPTEMBER 3
First of three articles
by Maria McGuire appears in *Observer*.

### SEPTEMBER 7
Two Protestants die in fight with British Paras in Belfast.

### SEPTEMBER 25
Whitelaw opens talks on future of Ireland at Darlington.

### OCTOBER 5
UDA conducts raid across border into Twenty-six Counties.

### OCTOBER 6
Twenty-six Counties police close Provisionals' Kevin Street office.

### OCTOBER 16
Four Protestant youths killed in clashes
with British Army in Belfast.

### OCTOBER 24
The 159th British soldier or UDR man to die, shot in Belfast.

### NOVEMBER 19
Sean Mac Stiofain arrested, begins hunger and thirst strike.

### NOVEMBER 25
Dublin Special Criminal Court
sentences Mac Stiofain to six months.

NOVEMBER 26
Attempt to rescue Mac Stiofain from Mater Hospital, Dublin,
foiled; bomb injures 25 in Dublin cinema.

NOVEMBER 27
Mac Stiofain transferred to the Curragh.

NOVEMBER 28
Provisionals fire Russian-made rockets
at British Army in Six Counties.

DECEMBER 1
Two die, 140 injured, in two bomb explosions in Dublin;
IRA denies responsibility.

DECEMBER 2
Offences against the State (Amendment) Act,
directed against IRA, passed in Dail by 70 votes to 23.

DECEMBER 7
Referendum ends Catholic Church's "special position"
in 1937 Constitution.